Coyote
True

THE NATHAN T. RIGGINS
WESTERN ADVENTURE SERIES
(Ages 9–12)

The Dog Who Would Not Smile
Coyote True

Coyote True

Stephen Bly

CROSSWAY BOOKS • WHEATON, ILLINOIS
A DIVISION OF GOOD NEWS PUBLISHERS

Published by Crossway Books, a division of Good News Publishers, 1300 Crescent St., Wheaton, Illinois 60187.

Cover illustration: David Yorke

First printing, 1992

Printed in the United States of America

For a list of other books by Stephen Bly or information regarding speaking engagements, write: Stephen Bly, Winchester, ID 83555.

Library of Congress Cataloging-in-Publication Data
Bly, Stephen A., 1944-
    Coyote True / by Stephen Bly.
        p.   cm. — (The Nathan T. Riggins western adventure series : bk. 2)
    Summary: In nineteenth-century Nevada, during a trip to round up cattle, twelve-year-old Nathan calls on God for help in dealing with hungry coyotes, an escaped outlaw, and injuries to his friends.
    [1. Frontier and pioneer life—Nevada—Fiction.
2. Nevada—Fiction. 3. West (U.S.)—Fiction. 4. Christian life—Fiction.] I. Title. II. Series: Bly, Stephen A., 1944-   Nathan T. Riggins western adventure series : bk. 2.
PZ7.B6275C1 1992   [Fic]—dc20   92-8224
ISBN 0-89107-680-8

00	99	98	97	96	95	94	93	92
15	14	13	12	11	10	9	8	7	6	5	4	3	2	1

For
Michelle Brewster

Ride 'em,
cowgirl

1

*H*ey, Nathan!" Leah called as she bounded up the wooden sidewalk. "Junior said he's gonna have his dog beat up your dog!" She brushed her brown bangs back and shaded her eyes.

Nathan T. Riggins of Galena, Nevada, tossed the old broom back into the marshal's office and sprinted towards Leah Walker. "Where is he?" he shouted.

"Out back, behind the bank looking for Tona!" she cried as they both ducked down the alley beside the Galena Store.

"Hurry!" Nathan gasped as he panted past Leah. "If we don't get there first, we'll have to bury a dog!"

Colin Maddison, Jr., (with two *d*'s) owned the largest dog Nathan had ever seen. While Colin Maddison, Sr., (also spelled with two *d*'s) ran the town's only bank, "Junior," as Leah and Nathan called him, tried to enforce his will on the entire population, and especially on Nathan and Leah.

The only thing that kept Colin Maddison, Jr., (with two *d*'s) from suffering bodily revenge was a hundred-pound Great Dane whom he called Sir Albert. The dog, always kept on a chain leash, dragged Junior throughout the city on a regular basis terrorizing the city animals and small children.

The sky was cloudless, and the sun reflected wildly off mud puddles that lay sprinkled across Main Street. September rains had turned the summer dust into autumn mud.

Tona never comes into town except at supper time. Or if I call him! Why is Junior such a jerk?

Nathan and Leah darted behind the row of outhouses and puffed up the hill. He carried his wide-brim hat in his hand.

"Junior! Junior! Wait! Wait up!" Nathan screamed. "Don't do it!"

Colin Maddison, Jr., (with two *d*'s) yanked back on the leash and spun around to face Nathan and Leah who had stopped to catch their breath fifty feet below.

"It's all over, Riggins! Say good-bye to that mangy mutt of yours. Sir Albert is hungry!"

"Wait!" Nathan gasped, as he struggled to catch up.

"I put up with you two ruffians all I'm going to. I'll teach you to trifle with me!" Colin threatened.

"What do you mean, trifle?" Leah doubled up at the waist trying to catch her breath.

"You two know exactly what I mean! And I've had about all of it I can take!" Junior warned.

When Nathan reached the top of the hill, he could see Sir Albert straining at the chain leash, growling and snapping his teeth at Tona who sat about twelve feet away, almost ignoring the confrontation.

"Wait, Junior!" Leah called again. "What did we do?"

"Well, to begin with, you never call me by my name!"

"What?" Nathan pressed, "Is that all that's wrong?"

"Okay," Leah offered, "we'll call you Colin. Don't let the dog get hurt!"

"My name is Colin Maddison, Jr., (with two *d*'s)."

"You mean we have to say all of that?" Nathan asked.

"Precisely. That is my name!"

Leah tilted her head, letting her long brown hair droop to the right. "What's precisely?"

"He said it was his name," Nathan responded.

Leah burst out laughing. "Is that precisely with two *p*'s?"

"That did it! You have tormented me long enough." Junior began to untie the leash.

"Wait!" Nathan shouted. "Look, Colin, see, I called you Colin. Leah's right. We'll call you Colin. We didn't know you didn't like Junior. I mean, you're always reminding us about the junior part."

"From now on you will call me Colin Maddison, Jr., (with two *d*'s). If you don't, I'll turn Sir Albert on that sorry excuse for a dog."

Junior was almost toppled off his feet by the Great Dane tugging at the chain. By now Nathan noticed that Tona had actually turned his head away from the others and was staring out across the Great Basin of northern Nevada. But the gray-white dog kept one ear perked to the conversation, especially the part coming from Sir Albert.

"We have to do what?" Leah groaned.

"Look, Colin," Nathan spouted, "Galena doesn't have a good side of town. So why don't you stop trying to pretend that you live over there and the rest of us are dirt?"

"The name is Colin Maddison, Jr., (with two *d*'s)!" he corrected.

"Oh, man, forget it." Nathan shrugged. "Turn the dog loose."

"What?" Leah screamed. "What about Tona?"

"Tona will kill Sir Albert, but that's Junior's choice," Nathan offered.

"Tona?" Junior waved his fist. "That worthless mixed breed will be dead in sixty seconds!"

"Look," Nathan explained, "I don't know what Sir Albert has been up against except little kids and cats, but Tona doesn't back away from snakes, bears, or men with rifles!

Don't go home crying." He jammed his gray cowboy hat back on his head.

"You're trying to bluff me again." Colin had taken the leash off the dog and held him only by the collar.

"If that dog attacks, Tona will kill it. He doesn't fight, except for his life, and then he never loses."

"Sic him, Sir Albert!" Junior released the Great Dane.

Leah screamed.

Junior chuckled.

Nathan sighed.

Sir Albert charged.

Tona whipped around toward the big dog, hunched down low, bared his teeth, and let go with a piercing, vicious growl that sent chills down Nathan's back.

He's going to kill Sir Albert!

The big dog pulled up three feet in front of Tona and stood, petrified. No barking. No growling. No forward movement. He stared at Tona's one white eye and one black eye.

Still in the hunched position, Tona leaned forward at Sir Albert and growled even louder.

Suddenly, the big dog spun around and flew down the hill towards town, almost knocking over Junior in his retreat.

"Sir Albert!" Junior cried. "Come back here and fight, you worthless coward!"

"Look at that!" Leah called.

"Sir Albert's smarter than I thought." Nathan took a deep breath and relaxed.

"I can't believe this," Junior pouted.

"Oh, come on, Junior. Tona's an Indian dog, you know."

"I didn't know that," Leah said.

"Will you two still call me Colin?" Junior sniffled.

"If that's what you want. But none of that two *d*'s stuff," Nathan offered.

Junior started to walk back down the hill with the others. "Even at school?"

"We will call you Colin at school, at church, and even in the bank. I like the name Colin." Leah smiled. "After all, I ain't never going to marry nobody except—"

"Yeah, yeah, we know," protested Nathan.

"Eh, in the bank you can call me Junior," Colin broke in. "I mean, that's what I'm called when I'm in Father's bank."

"O.K." Nathan trudged down the hill leading the other two.

"And when you're over at my house, always call me Junior when my mother's around," Colin added.

"Whatever you say. But listen," Nathan cautioned, "don't tease Tona again. He'll protect himself with vengeance."

"Is he really an Indian dog?" Colin asked.

"Yep. He once belonged to Pie-a-ra-poo'-na's grandson." Nathan stuck his face right into the other boy's. "He's the chief of the To-na-wits'-o-wa Shoshone."

Colin's eyes grew large, and he stopped and stared back up the hill towards Tona.

Nathan's dog was nowhere in sight.

■

For almost fifteen minutes Nathan stared into the mirror. He was trying to imagine what he would look like with a mustache. Of course, he would have to wait several years to find out.

I need to grow. If I were just six inches taller and maybe a little stronger, and if my front teeth weren't so crooked, and if my nose were a little smaller . . . Lord, are You sure You didn't make any mistakes here?

He finished combing his sandy brown hair and scooted onto the back bench by the table where his mother had a plate of biscuits and gravy waiting for him.

"Are you going to work at the store after school?" she asked.

"I don't think they need any more help. Have you noticed that fewer and fewer new people are coming to town?" he offered.

Mrs. Riggins pulled on her long coat and gathered up a plate of food. "I'm taking this over to your father at the office."

"Did he lock up someone else last night?" Nathan asked.

"Yes, and Deputy Haley is over in Austin. So Father did guard duty. You'll need to get yourself out the door in time for school. Your lunch bucket is there on the counter. Be good and—"

"I know, I know," Nathan said laughing. "Be good and learn something new. Mother, you say that every morning."

"Well, I don't want you to forget what school's all about." She walked over and hugged Nathan's shoulder and kissed him on the ear. Then she gathered up the dishes and floated out the front door.

A year ago Nathan Riggins would have protested when his mother hugged and kissed him. Twelve years is just too old for that sort of stuff, he had figured. But the past few months of being separated from his mother and father, of being lost in this wild country and finally finding his parents again made him see things differently.

She can hug me anytime she wants—as long as no one sees it!

School was held in the back room of the Welsh Miner's

Hall. It was a small room but always warm and clean, thanks to Miss Aimee Bryce, the teacher. There were eight students, ranging in age from five to twelve. Miss Bryce had scattered the pupils around the room in no apparent order and refused to tell them what grades they were in.

"Everyone can work at his or her own level," she announced with a broad smile. In the few weeks of school, Leah had begun to read a few words, and Nathan had started studying Latin.

Nathan thought that Miss Bryce just might be the most beautiful woman on earth. That's why he had spent fifteen minutes wishing in the mirror for a mustache.

If I were just a little bit older!

Even though he left promptly and walked straight to school, Leah had arrived before him.

"How come you're always here so early?" he asked.

"'Cause I help Miss Bryce straighten up the room, that's why!" she sassed. "Besides, I need more help. This is only the second year I ever gone to school, and I don't remember nothin' from the other one."

"Where's Miss Bryce?" Nathan looked around the little room.

"Well, she's just not here yet!" Leah informed him. "Maybe she's baking us a treat. She sure can cook good."

"But she's never late!" Nathan walked over to the wood stove and noticed that it was cold. About that time Colin pushed through the door with a couple of the younger children behind him.

"Where's Miss Bryce?" he called. "I've got to give her a note from my mother."

Propped up on the middle of Miss Bryce's desk was a large envelope. Nathan stared at it and then grabbed it up. "Hey, here's a note. Maybe she's sick or something." The others gathered to the front as Nathan unfolded the stiff linen paper. He began to read the letter out loud.

Dear Class,

Someday when all of you grow up (and I'm sure you will be fine men and women), you will understand why I'm doing something so drastic.

Late tonight, I had a visit from Joshua Boyd. You may remember that I mentioned a gentleman who was herding cattle near here, and we had been childhood friends. Well, to come right to the point, and this is very difficult to say, Mr. Boyd asked me to travel to Virginia City and marry him. And I said yes.

It was necessary for me to leave this very evening. I don't blame you for being angry with me for abandoning you, but I'm sure the fine folks of Galena will be able to find another teacher. At twenty years old, I was not all that confident I would receive another offer.

I love you all. Please forgive me.

Yours truly,
Miss Aimee Bryce

"But she can't do that!" Colin protested. "She has a contract! She didn't even tell my father!"

"We don't have a teacher?" One of the little children started to cry.

"Uh, well, I guess," Nathan stammered, "it's sort of like a vacation. Don't worry; they'll get us a new teacher."

"But I don't want a new teacher! I want Miss Bryce," a child whined.

Only Leah seemed to understand.

"I wish I could go to Miss Bryce's wedding," she said wistfully. "She would sure look pretty in a long wedding dress! When I grow up, I'm gonna look just like Miss Bryce."

Nathan ran all the way to his father's office carrying the note.

"Dad!" he yelled down the sidewalk. "Dad! Mom!" He burst into the marshal's office. "Miss Bryce ran off to get married, and we ain't got no teacher!"

"We don't have a teacher," his mother corrected.

"What are we going to do?" Nathan puffed.

"Well, that explains Josh Boyd's scribbled note."

"They really did it, didn't they?" Mrs. Riggins added.

"I suppose we should have seen it coming." Marshal Riggins nodded. "Josh was courtin' every weekend for a month."

"But really they have only known each other since July." Mrs. Riggins stood up and walked across the room, closing the door behind Nathan.

"But they knew each other years ago," Mr. Riggins offered.

"What are we going to do?" Nathan repeated.

"Well," his father said pondering, "first, let's make sure all the children get back home this morning. Adele, could you see that the parents know what's going on?"

"Certainly."

"Then I'll tell the mayor, and I suppose they will send a wire to Austin and ask that another teacher be sent up."

Nathan paced the floor. "How long will that take?"

"A month, six months—who knows?" His father

shrugged. "Anyway you look at it, you're going to miss some school."

"But what about Latin? And arithmetic . . . and grammar . . . what about—"

"Nathan, you'll just have to wait a while to learn all those things," his mother cautioned.

"Nate, I'll need you to guard the prisoners while I go find the mayor."

"Will he be all right, David?" Mrs. Riggins pressed.

"I've got the only key with me." He grabbed Nathan around the shoulders. "Besides, this young man traveled across the country by himself—fought off snakes, bears, outlaws, and dust storms. He should have no trouble with a couple of drunks who are sleeping it off."

■

Nathan liked spending time in his father's office. There was a drawer full of "wanted" posters to look at, a locker full of rifles, and newspapers from all over the state.

He had just finished reading about how two fourteen-year-old boys in Paradise Valley were arrested for holding up a stagecoach. Then his father returned.

"Okay, Nate, you can head home. Hey, listen!" His dad paused and turned. "How would you like to cowboy for a week or so?"

"What? You really mean it—with cows?" Nathan stammered.

"Yep. That's what a cowboy does. You see, Josh Boyd was looking after a hundred head of cows and and their calves for the mayor and several other men in town. Well, now that he ran off to marry the schoolteacher, someone's got to go up into the mountains and drive them to town for the winter."

"Who's going to do it?"

"You and me," his dad replied. "What do you say?"

"You're not kidding?"

"Nope."

"How come they asked you? Is it the marshal's job?"

His dad laughed. "Not hardly, but they offered me three cows when I bring them in. So I figured it's our chance to get a start in the cattle business. Besides, Deputy Haley can handle things here."

"How long will we be gone?"

"About four or five days, depending on the roundup. It's not all that far."

"Can I go tell Mom?" Nathan asked.

"How about you going to ask her permission?"

"But what if she says no?" Nathan moaned.

"What if she doesn't?"

"Yeah! Thanks, Dad." Nathan ran to the door and then turned. "Hey, Dad, listen, could I ask a friend to come with us? I mean, since there's no school anyway."

"We'll talk about it over dinner," Marshal Riggins concluded.

Nathan ran down the sidewalk, spun around in front of the Wild Horse Cantina, and then raced back into his father's office.

"Dad, Dad! Hey, Dad! Do I get to wear a pistol? Cowboys always pack iron."

"'Pack iron?' Where do you hear terms like that?"

"You know, in *Frank Leslie's Illustrated Weekly*," Nathan admitted.

"No, you may not 'pack iron.' But you can stick your

rifle in the scabbard. We might stumble across a coyote up there."

Again Nathan ran for home. Leah spotted him and tried to keep up. "Nathan, where are you going?"

"I'm going to cowboy, that's what!"

2

Nevada winds blow cold in late September. In the north central part of the state a series of mountain ranges run north and south with wide, dry, sage-covered valleys in between.

Seldom is there a tree, even in the mountains. But there *is* plenty of dust.

Nathan pulled his tattered gray hat low, trying to keep the dirt out of his eyes as he saddled his horse. His father had refused to let him take Mr. Dawson's horse, Ace, to the mountains, insisting that he needed a cow pony instead.

So Nathan now threw the blanket over the back of a fourteen-and-a-half-hand sorrel gelding called Copper and struggled to set the saddle. Finally, having yanked the cinches tight, he fastened a coiled thirty-foot maguey rope to a thin strip of leather and looped it over the horn.

Still fighting dust, he rerolled his blankets and extra clothing, wrapping his slicker around the outside. Tying the whole roll behind his cantle, he rechecked his canteen and then drooped it from the saddle horn as well. Finally, he slipped his varmint-hunting rifle into the scabbard.

Leading the horse by the reins, Nathan walked up the crowded dirt street towards the marshal's office. He could have ridden the two blocks, but he wanted to hear the music of the jingle-bobs dangling from his new spurs.

"Nathan, where did you get all that cowboy gear?" Leah Walker called out to him.

"Uh, this stuff? You know—here and there," he blustered as he noticed several men standing on the sidewalk, listening to the conversation.

Leah ran up to him. "Nathan, why won't you let me come?"

"I told you, Leah, you can't go because you're a girl."

"Well, I can ride a horse just as good as you can, Nathan T. Riggins!"

"It's going to be cold up there." Nathan kept walking towards the marshal's office.

"I got a coat, and you know I got good shoes. Don't I have good shoes?" she pressed.

"Yes, yes, but my mother said it's just not proper for a young lady to travel unchaperoned with men."

Leah curled her lip. "Your daddy will be there, right?"

"Well, yes, but still—"

"But nothin'. If you or Junior ever got fresh with me, I'd bust every tooth in your mouth. You know that, don't ya?"

"Sure, but you see—"

"Besides," Leah cried, "I ain't no lady, and you ain't no man. So why can't I go? You did tell your mom that I ain't never goin' to marry nobody but Kylie Colins, didn't you?"

"I told her." Nathan hitched Copper to the rail in front of the marshal's office.

"Nathan, does your momma hate me?" Leah brushed some dirt off her long dark blue dress.

"No! Of course not! It's just that, well, she's afraid you'll get hurt or something." Nathan patted Copper's neck.

"I could get hurt here in Galena," Leah protested. "You saw what happened to Jimmy Peters's leg when he got run over by a freight wagon. And that was right over by the gate to the

Shiloh Mine. I'd probably be safer up in the mountains with the cows than down here in town. I'm going to go talk with your momma."

"Leah," Nathan said sighing, "you can't go with us. That's all there is to it! Besides, my mother left this morning on the stage to Battle Mountain Station to meet some cousin who's coming in on the train."

Leah turned back up the street, wrapping her arms around her shoulders to keep warm and mumbling under her breath.

When he entered the office, his dad was busy giving instructions to an older man known around town only as Pepper. The man was extremely tall and very thin. Most of the kids nicknamed him "Old Flagpole."

"Nate! Good. You're here." His dad nodded toward Pepper. "Listen, a wire came in that the judge is coming to town tomorrow morning. Something about an escaped prisoner. So I'll have to stick around one more day."

"You mean, we aren't leaving until tomorrow?" Nathan moaned. "But I'm all loaded up!"

"No, I didn't say you had to wait until tomorrow. Pepper has agreed to go with you two today. I'll catch up by tomorrow night late. You can pitch camp at the cabin and patch that box canyon corral. No reason for all of you to wait on me. Pepper will cook for us and help drive the cows back to town."

"But, Dad," Nathan protested, looking at Pepper, "we don't even know how to find the place!"

Rubbing his shaggy black and gray beard, Pepper looked at Nathan. "How old are you, boy?"

"I'm twelve. Actually, I'm twelve and a half." Nathan took off his hat and held it as he spoke.

"Well, I'll be. Ya know, I was about your age when I rode with Sam Houston."

"You were with Houston?" Nathan gasped.

"Down at San Jacinto." Pepper smiled.

"The Battle of San Jacinto? You were in the Battle of San Jacinto?" Nathan shook his head with amazement.

"Son, old Pepper's been up and down purt' near every trail between California and Kansas." Then turning to Nathan's father, he asked, "David, did I ever tell you about the time I was sheriff of Abilene?"

"Abilene, Kansas?" Nathan interjected.

"Yep. For two nights and three days. Then they fired me."

"Fired you?"

"Well, it's a long story. I'll go get the gear loaded into the wagon and meet you over in front of the hotel. We'll have plenty of time for stories once we get out on the trail."

Pepper limped to the door and disappeared down the sidewalk.

"Is he hurt?" Nathan asked.

"Said he got kicked by a horse just yesterday evening. How about it, Nate? You can head on out with Pepper or wait around town until tomorrow."

"Did he really fight with Sam Houston?"

"As far as I know." His dad grinned. "Then I presume you don't mind traveling with Pepper?"

"Oh, yeah, sure. I mean, you'll catch up tomorrow. We could use his help cooking," he added.

Suddenly the office door banged open, and Colin Maddison, Jr., (with two *d*'s) swaggered into the room wearing the bushiest woolly chaps Nathan had ever seen.

"Junior! I mean, Colin." Nathan tried to keep from laughing. "Where did you get those?"

"These happen to be a present from my uncle. He purchased them in old Mexico."

"You look like you're wearing a sheep on each leg!" Nathan hooted. "Did you gut them out first or just jam your foot right into the mouth?"

"Actually, they are quite comfortable!" Colin insisted.

"Well," Marshal Riggins added, "be sure the coyotes don't attack your leg and carry you off to their den."

Colin swallowed hard. "Are there really coyotes up there?"

"Yep. But don't pester them. 'Course, if they start grabbing calves, you'll have to shoot them."

Colin's eyes grew wide. "Shoot them? You mean with a gun?"

"Yep." Marshal Riggins turned and winked at Nathan. "Okay, son, you got your gear packed and loaded on your horse, and you kissed your momma good-bye. I guess you're all set."

"Yes, sir."

The marshal walked over and put his arms around the shoulders of both boys. "Well, you cowboys take it easy on old Pepper. He's a good hand, but he won't cut any slack with a couple of colts. Be careful now. I'll be seein' you on down the trail."

Nathan and Colin mounted up and rode towards the hotel with Nathan explaining the new circumstances. Pepper was tying the load in the back of a wagon hitched to two stout mules.

"Well," Pepper growled, "did you kiss your Marys good-bye?"

"W-w-what?" Colin stammered.

"No matter. It's time to roll." With some obvious pain Pepper pulled himself up into the wagon seat and slapped the long lead against the mule's rump. The team and wagon lurched forward. Nathan and Colin pulled in behind, fighting off the dust with their hats jerked low and their jacket collars turned high.

They had just rattled north past Moon's Saloon and the Rocky Acres Cemetery when Nathan heard someone holler at him from the direction of town.

"Wait! Nathan! Colin! Wait for me!"

Leah came riding up on a white mare loaded with gear.

"What are you doing?" Colin asked.

Pepper, not knowing the boys had halted, kept the wagon rolling north.

"I'm going with you," Leah announced.

"You can't!" Nathan pulled off his hat and scratched the back of his head. "I told you you couldn't."

"I know what you told me, Nathan T. Riggins, and it's just not fair. So I packed up my outfit, and I'm coming."

"We won't let you," Colin declared.

"Oh yeah, how would you like a broken nose, Junior?" she threatened. "Besides, this ain't no toll road, so I can go on it if I want to."

"Does your father know you're coming?" Nathan asked.

"My father is in Austin looking for another wife," Leah said nodding. "So I can do anything I want."

"Another wife?" Colin queried.

"Yeah, the last one ran off in June, so he needs a new one."

"You really can't come with us. My dad said—" Nathan began.

"Well, your daddy ain't here, is he? So you just ride up there and tell Old Flagpole that you forgot to mention that I was comin' too."

"I can't do that!" Nathan protested.

"Well, why not?"

"'Cause it's a lie. Leah, I don't think this is going to work," Nathan insisted.

She kicked her horse and trotted on ahead of the boys, still quite a distance from the wagon. "Nathan Riggins, I don't see why it's such a nuisance for you to take me along. Besides, it ain't a big lie . . . it's just a baby lie."

"A what?" Colin bounced along on his horse, trying to keep up with the conversation.

"Baby lies don't hurt no one. God don't care about baby lies—right, Nathan?"

"Actually, I think He—"

"Anyway, it's my decision, not yours, so I'll just trail along. Pepper won't send me home alone in the dark."

"What are we going to tell Pepper?" Colin wondered.

"What are we going to tell Dad?" Nathan moaned.

"Boys, it ain't nothin' important. Come on!" Leah kicked her horse and hurried to catch up with the wagon. To Nathan's surprise she rode right up to the side of the wagon and started a conversation with Pepper.

"Miss Leah, what are you doin' out here?" Pepper called.

Nathan rode close enough to hear.

"Well, my daddy had important business down in Austin, and I didn't have no one to stay with. So Nathan was worried about me and said that no girl should have to be on her own in a town like Galena. He said I could tag along with you all, providin' I would pull my own freight and not be a bother."

"That's right noble of him." Pepper scratched his beard. "But still, taking a girl to drive cattle . . . it just ain't right."

"Nathan," Pepper yelled, "how come the marshal didn't mention a female coming on the trip?"

Leah turned back to Nathan, her eyes pleading.

"Well . . . I . . . I, eh, I didn't have time to ask my dad. See, it just seemed like the right thing to do. But, but . . . if you think it's wrong—"

"Of course he don't think it's wrong." Leah smiled. "Do you, Pepper?"

"Well, it's just that I don't—"

"Oh," Leah bubbled, "did I ever tell you that my Grandpa Hall was at the Alamo?"

"You don't say? With Col. Travis when he, Bowie, Crockett, and the others went down?"

"Oh, yes. By the way, weren't you down in Texas in the olden days?" she questioned.

"Olden days?" He laughed. "Well, you're right about that, little lady. Spent many a night chasing old Santa Anna or running from him."

"I was born in Texas, but my daddy moved up here when I was only two. What's Texas like? Is it pretty? I always dreamed that it was a very beautiful country."

"Well, you're right about that, Miss Leah. When those bluebonnets are bloomin' and the hill country is green, it's purt' near Heaven."

Oh brother, Nathan moaned to himself. *She's got him hoodwinked. Lord, what should I do now? She really wants to go, and, well, she ought to do more than just sit in town waiting for her dad to bring home another woman.*

"Are we going to let her pull that off?" Colin demanded.

"She's determined to come along. What can we do?" Nathan shrugged.

"Well, I'm certainly not sharing my tea and cakes with her," Colin announced.

"No, I don't suppose you will." Nathan pulled his bandana up on his face to keep the dust out of his mouth.

"Look, Nathan!" Colin pointed. "There's your dog!"

Glancing to the south, Nathan saw Tona scoot through

the sage about twenty feet to the west of the wagon. He whistled, and Tona trotted over to the sorrel horse and looked up at him.

"Tona, you go up there and run ahead of the wagon. Scout it out. We don't want any surprises!" he ordered the dog.

"That dog doesn't have the foggiest idea what you are talking about," Colin lectured.

Nathan ignored the comment and watched as Tona slipped back out into the sage, sprinted by the wagon, and began loping along ahead of the mules.

"How did you get him to do that?" Colin mumbled through his bandana.

"Easy . . . always ask a dog to do what he's planning on doing anyway," Nathan advised.

Within an hour, Pepper stopped the wagon, tied Leah's horse to the back, and allowed her to ride next to him. It was noon before they stopped again.

Old Flagpole had pulled the wagon off the road and cut overland to a small spring that wandered down a narrow ravine.

"Well, boys—and young lady, all we have is a little hardtack and beans for dinner. Everything else is boxed up. Miss Leah and I will kick a fire goin', and you two see that all the horses are watered."

"Thank you for watering my horse," she teased Nathan as he brought the horses back and tied them to the wagon.

"Look . . . you're here—so far. But what about pulling your own freight?" he griped. "You've got to do your share, or we'll turn the wagon around and go home."

For a minute Leah stared right into Nathan's eyes. He felt uncomfortable and wanted to glance down.

But he didn't.

"Well, you're right," she finally said. "I'm sorry for acting kind of, you know . . . snotty."

"Okay, hombres," Pepper called out, "let's get hitched up and on the trail. We need to hit that cabin before dark. There's a coyote wind stirring up."

"A coyote wind?" Colin asked.

"Yep. About a day before a fierce storm hits, the coyotes all get a little nervous. Mark my words, they will be howling before the moon comes out."

The road got steeper.

The wind stiffer.

The temperature colder.

And the saddle harder.

The sun had long since set, and the crimson western sky turned charcoal before the wagon rolled down a narrow trail leading up a side canyon and stopped in front of a tiny log cabin tucked against a sheer rock wall.

Even before he climbed off Copper, Nathan heard the howl of a nearby coyote.

3

Nathan didn't know exactly when it happened. He had fed the horses and turned them into the corral. Then he helped unload the wagon and stacked all the supplies inside. Finally, he hiked out back to bring in an arm load of wood.

That's when he looked up and noticed them. Thousands of bright twinkling stars appeared all at once. Like wildflowers sprinkled across a green mountain meadow, the stars clustered thick in the black heavens. The steady wind of the afternoon had slacked, and the temperature was dropping.

"Nathan! Hey, Nathan!" Leah broke his silence. "There's some hot supper in here. What you doin' holding that wood?"

"Oh . . . just looking at the stars. Leah, did you know those stars have names?"

"I wonder if one of them is named Leah."

"Of course not. They have funny names that the Greeks gave them a long time ago."

Leah put her hands on her hips and tilted her head. "Do you know all the names of the stars?"

Nathan walked toward the cabin. "No, of course not!"

"Well, then," she scolded, "how do you know there ain't one star named Leah? See that one over there? The bright one? Well, I believe its name is Leah!"

"That's not a star . . . it's a planet," Nathan instructed. "The stars all blink, but the planets give off a steady light."

"Nope. You're wrong. That's the famous star, Leah!" She spun on her heels and entered the cabin.

Nathan followed right behind.

The summer cabin was about ten feet wide and fifteen feet long with a crumbling rock fireplace at one end. Inside was one bunk with rawhide lacings for a mattress, a broken chair, and three log rounds that looked like stools. If there had ever been a table, it had long since disappeared. Occasional nails in the log walls presented the only thing close to a storage shelf.

Huddled near the fire, which gave out only moderate heat, the quartet ate their supper and stared into the flames.

It was Pepper who broke the silence. "There's only one thing missing from this cabin."

"One?" Colin moaned. "How about no kitchen sink, no tub, no decent chair, no cookstove, no—"

Nathan, not knowing how long Colin would go on, interrupted him. "Pepper, what's missing?"

"Mice."

"Mice?" Leah murmured. "We need mice?"

"Nope." Pepper took his long knife and cleaned a piece of meat out from between his front teeth. "We don't need mice, but there ought to be some mice here. Every line camp I ever set foot in had a nest or two of mice. But you look around here and you can't find even a dropping."

"Is that bad?" Nathan asked.

"I don't like mice," Colin chimed in.

"Well," Pepper said smiling, "what it means is, something has been eating the mice."

"Like a cat?" Nathan quizzed.

"Could be . . . or maybe a snake!" A big grin broke across Pepper's bearded face.

"Snakes?" Leah moaned. "I'm scared of snakes!"

"Now, Miss Leah, I didn't say that there are snakes. But it would surprise me if we don't discover some kind of mouse-eater around here."

No more was mentioned about snakes until it was time to roll out the bedrolls and go to sleep.

"I'm sleeping on the cot," Leah announced.

"You?" Colin griped. "Look, I think we should draw lots for the cot. I don't exactly cherish the idea of sleeping down here with the . . . I mean, down here on the floor."

"Tona's good at killing snakes," Nathan offered.

"Well, why not let him stay in the cabin with us?" Leah suggested.

"Oh, he never goes into buildings," Nathan reported.

"Don't you worry about snakes." Pepper shrugged. "They're probably gettin' all holed up for the winter anyway. Miss Leah, we'll shove that cot down at the far end, and that will be your quarters. Sorry you don't get a private room, but we didn't know you were going to be with us."

As he was rolling out his blanket, Nathan heard Tona barking out in the yard between the cabin and the corral.

"Something's out there," he cautioned. "Tona never barks except for trouble."

"Snakes," Colin moaned, "we're going to be eaten by rattlesnakes!"

"Not snakes," Pepper informed him. "They'd stay where it's warm. Probably just a skunk—or a porcupine or a coyote."

"Do coyotes eat mice?" Leah asked from under the blankets on top of her cot.

"Yep." Pepper stirred the fire and pulled a soiled, four-point blanket around his shoulders. "They eat anything they can sink their teeth into. Never seen a coyote yet that wasn't half-starved."

31

Nathan tried to find a comfortable position on the floor, rolling first on one side and then on the other. It reminded him of early summer when he had slept out on Big Belle Mountain. What bothered him most was Tona's sporadic barking. He had tried to shout the dog quiet, but Tona wasn't listening.

■

"What's that?" Leah shouted.

"What?" Nathan mumbled, trying to remember where he was.

"I heard something eating! They're near my bed too! The snakes are chewing up mice right under my bed!" She panicked.

"Snakes don't chew," Nathan mumbled. "They just swallow it whole, right, Colin?"

There was no answer.

"Colin!"

"Uwf . . . swop . . . nasna . . . "

"What? What did he say?" Leah pressed.

"Colin, are you eating something?" Nathan accused.

"I said," Colin swallowed hard, "that I don't hear anything."

"You were eating those sweet cakes, weren't you?" Nathan demanded.

"What if I was? My mother purchased them for me, and I didn't think it polite to eat in front of others," he explained.

"Well, you should be unselfish enough to share them with us," Nathan rebuked him.

"You're not only making us hungry, but you're keeping us awake by crunching on them," Leah complained.

Suddenly Pepper sat straight up on the floor, and his

shadow from the fireplace light flickered menacingly on the cabin wall. "The next one, the very next one of you to sound off at the mouth will be bodily thrown out the front door and forced to sleep with the mules! Is that understood?"

Neither Nathan, nor Leah, nor Colin spoke another word.

■

It was not at all the best night Nathan had ever had, and he rolled out of bed as soon as he saw Old Flagpole stirring the fire. Nathan rubbed his eyes and struggled to pull on his boots.

"Mornin', Pepper," he greeted him. "Are we going to round up the cows and calves today?"

"Nope. We'll wait for your daddy to get up here for that. We've got to patch up that fence today. Pull on your coat and go out there and check on the horses," Pepper instructed. "And see if you can find out why that flea bag of yours barked all night."

Nathan was surprised to discover that it was a dark, cloudy morning. The sky that had been decorated with stars hours before now crouched low with draping black clouds.

Coyote winds, Old Flagpole called them. Well, there sure is a storm rolling in, but I didn't hear any coyotes. 'Course, I couldn't have heard anything but Tona anyway.

In the daylight Nathan could see the broken-down fence. The small corral where they had turned out the horses and mules was fairly stout, but no larger than a round pen used for breaking horses.

The east fence line that sealed off the box canyon leaned at a forty-five degree angle, needing only another snow storm to drive it to the ground. Its only gate was sagging so badly that Nathan couldn't close it. Several top rails were broken out, and a few were missing altogether.

"Man, what did Joshua Boyd do up here all summer?" Nathan mumbled. "Dreamed about Miss Bryce, I suppose. Don't guess I can blame him for that." *Lord, look, this is Nathan. I was wondering, You know, later on, say in six or eight years . . . if you had another Miss Bryce around somewhere, well, maybe I could—*

His thoughts began to embarrass him, and Nathan looked around for Tona. The gray and white dog was crouching about thirty feet straight west of the far end of the cabin. His tail started to wag when he heard Nathan's voice, but he wouldn't take his eyes off the cabin.

"Tona," Nathan blurted out, "what happened to you?" He examined a scratch that started near Tona's left eye, stretched down his long nose, and crossed over to the right side, ending near his mouth. "What is it, boy? What's over by the cabin? A bobcat? Did you tangle with a cat?"

Tona stood to his feet, but never took his eyes off the cabin. Nathan heard the dog's low growl that signaled his expectation of an attack.

Walking closer to the cabin to search for clues, Nathan noticed that Tona crouched at his side for several steps, then hunched down in a fighting position, and began barking.

Looking closely, Nathan could see a hole dug in the dirt under the cabin floor behind two small sagebrush plants that struggled for survival.

"A lair? What's in there? Is there a skunk in there or something? Oh, man, I hope it's not a skunk."

"What ya looking at?" Leah called from the front step.

"Trying to discover what's under the cabin. Some varmint ripped up Tona's nose. It's hiding under the cabin!"

"Under that end? That's right where my bunk is!" Leah howled. "It's the snakes! I told you that I heard snakes!"

"Snakes don't scratch dogs!" Nathan scoffed. "Besides, the hole is way too big."

"Wait. I want to get my coat!" Leah raced into the cabin and popped back out, pulling on her coat and carrying Nathan's rifle. "Here!" she panted. "Shoot it! Whatever it is, shoot it!"

Nathan took the rifle. "I'm not going to shoot anything!"

"Why not? It must be very dangerous if it hurt Tona."

"Maybe so, but you don't ever aim a gun at a cabin with people in it, and besides, there aren't any bullets in the rifle."

"No bullets?"

"Of course not. I don't usually go carrying this around on a horse all loaded up. If that horse has a blow-up, either him or me could catch a bullet. Didn't your father ever teach you anything about guns?"

"I'm a girl, and I don't have to learn nothin' about guns."

By now Nathan stood not more than three feet from the hole, trying to peer into the darkness under the cabin. Tona's barking was at the near panic level.

"Wouldn't get one step closer, if I was you," Pepper boomed from the yard.

Nathan looked up to see Old Flagpole, without his boots on, standing behind Leah. "What kind of varmint do you think it is?" Nathan asked.

"Read the signs." Pepper nodded.

"What?" Nathan tilted his head sideways and squinted his eyes.

"The tracks, boy! Look at the tracks."

"Oh." Nathan and Leah searched around the dirt next to the sagebrush. "Well, I don't see anything but Tona's prints."

"Dog, eh?" Pepper jammed his hands into the pockets of his dirty coat. "You know what that means, don't ya?"

"There's another dog in there?" Nathan asked.

"Boy, have you spent your whole life in a hotel? Them ain't dog prints. Coyotes. That's a coyote den, and your mutt done right well to escape with only a little scratch."

"Coyotes? Under my bed!" Leah squealed.

"What are we going to do about them?" Nathan asked Pepper.

"Nothin' yet," he replied. "If they get worried about us, they'll move on their own. Just don't go sticking your hand in there, and keep your dog at a safe distance."

Colin pranced barefoot outside the cabin, rubbing his eyes. "Look at those clouds. We certainly won't be able to work today in this kind of weather."

"What?" Pepper roared. "This is great fence-building weather. It'll keep us moving to stay warm. Couldn't ask for anything better!"

"Uh, Pepper," Leah asked, "what exactly do coyotes do down in a hole like that?"

"They raise their youngin's, that's what they do. Probably a litter of pups down there. Do you hear any yippin'?"

"Not really." Nathan shrugged.

"Well, that's good. They're probably all latched onto momma coyote."

"And where's the father?" Colin asked.

"Out there huntin' breakfast, I would imagine. Hope they don't plan on eating calf."

"They can kill calves?"

"Sure, that's their job."

"Their job?" Nathan questioned.

"Yep. Coyotes are supposed to act like coyotes. That means huntin' their dinner and bringing some home to the rest of the family. Being 'coyote true'—that's what it is. That's all we're doin' up here, ain't it? Bringing these cows and calves back to town to feed our families. That's *our* job."

"And what happens when coyotes try to steal our calves?" Nathan asked.

"We shoot 'em." Pepper smiled. "But we don't get mad at them."

"So we're just going to leave them in there?" Leah pointed at the hole.

"Yep. As long as Mr. Coyote don't bother me, I won't bother him." Pepper pulled on the boots he carried over his shoulder and turned to walk towards the tottering fence.

■

Old Flagpole turned out to be a good foreman even though he increasingly limped on his bad foot. By noon the gate had been re-set and most of the missing rails replaced. He and Nathan had started propping up the sagging fence line.

"Miss Leah," he pointed towards the cabin, "you and Colin go warm us up some dinner."

Just as they turned to head towards the cabin, Pepper halted them in their tracks. "Wait up! Nathan, grab that dog of yours!"

Without knowing what was going on, Nathan whistled and Tona ran to his side. He reached down and hugged Tona around the neck. Tona, enjoying the attention, faced Nathan and the others.

"Look up that draw over yonder," Pepper called out. "He's slinking up through the sage."

"It's a coyote!" Leah exclaimed.

"Shh! Don't spook him," Pepper warned. "Just watch."

The male coyote trotted from sage to sage, keeping hidden most of the time until he reached the west side of the cabin.

"Look," Nathan whispered, "there's another one coming out of the hole!"

"It must be the mother!" Leah tried to keep her voice low.

Suddenly the male made a low, hoarse coughing sound.

"He's sick. Oh, man," Colin gagged, "he vomited!"

"Regurgitated," Pepper corrected him.

"Disgusting!" Colin wrinkled his nose. "Look, look! That other one is eating it! I think I'm going to puke."

"No, it ain't disgusting," Pepper disagreed. "That's exactly what a coyote is supposed to do. They swallow the food nearly whole and then bring it home for the others. He's just feeding them—that's all."

"Eh . . ." Leah stammered, "I don't think I'm very hungry."

"Me neither!" Nathan added.

"I tell you, I'm going to lose my breakfast," Colin gagged.

Nathan thought Colin really looked green.

"Well, a fine crew I've got here!" Pepper laughed. "Okay, let's put in another hour before we stop for dinner."

In a matter of moments, they saw the male coyote slink away from the cabin and dart back into the sagebrush.

"He's headin' out for more victuals." Pepper nodded.

"Well, next time I'm sure not going to watch," Leah declared.

"Look!" Pepper motioned. "Those pups must be a hungry lot. Momma's going huntin' too!"

Nathan looked around to see a slightly smaller coyote emerge from the hole and trot down the hill.

"The puppies are all alone," Leah offered.

"Well, don't you go messin' with those pups," Pepper cautioned. "You'll get 'em all killed, you will."

4

Nathan and Pepper hitched one of the mules to a fence post and pulled it up straight. Then they jabbed a big rock into the open side of the post hole to keep it pointing skyward. Finally, they shoveled in loose dirt and tamped it tight.

Pepper limped along favoring his injured foot even more.

"You better rest that foot," Nathan advised.

"A little work is all it needs. I don't want it to stove up on me." Pepper spoke without much conviction.

Colin ran out to tell them dinner was ready.

"Dinner?" Pepper growled, "It's late enough to be supper! What did you two do, bake us a pie?"

"Eh no, we, ah, the fire went out," Colin mumbled.

■

By the middle of the afternoon they were back at the corral, continuing to shore up the fence.

"I don't suppose my dad will make it up here until after dark." Nathan stopped for a minute to button up his jacket. "I think it's getting colder."

"Well, at least it hasn't begun to rain," Leah said. "I thought for sure we'd be stormed on by now."

Colin, the only one with a watch, pulled it out of his

pocket and then turned to Pepper. "What time do we quit?" he asked.

"What time do we quit? You think you're working at your daddy's bank, boy?" Pepper blasted. "We quit when the job's done, that's when."

Colin changed the subject. "Nathan, how come you brought your gun out here after dinner?"

Nathan kept working as he talked. "Well, I was worried that Tona might have a run-in with those coyotes again. I just wanted to make sure it was an even fight."

"You wouldn't shoot the coyotes, would you?" Leah sounded distressed.

"Only if they were about to kill Tona. That dog pulled me out of the fire too many times to let him go it alone."

"Well said, son, well said," Pepper added. "Don't start no fight, but always stick up for your friends. Yes, sir, that's the way we do it."

The sun was just hanging at the mountaintop when they finished bracing the last post and Pepper announced it was quitting time.

"I have blisters all over my hands," Colin moaned. "My mother will be very displeased."

"I ain't got no momma, so I guess that makes me lucky, huh, Colin?" Leah pressed.

"Well, I only meant . . . hey, look, here come the coyotes!" Colin pointed to the cabin.

Both the male and the female slinked toward the hole with the female entering first. She immediately exited the hole carrying one of the squealing pups in her mouth.

"She's killing the puppy!" Leah cried.

"Nope, she's movin' it. I guess they don't like our company," Pepper explained.

"Where's she moving it to?" Leah questioned.

"Can't say, but probably someplace where we won't find them," Pepper added.

After the female and pup were out of sight, the male entered the hole.

"Hey," Nathan said pointing, "look, the daddy is going to carry one. No! He can't do that; he's breaking its neck; he's killing that pup!"

"Stop him, Nathan, stop him!" Leah screamed.

Nathan sprinted towards the corral gate where he had left his rifle leaning against the post.

"He's got another one," she cried. "Nathan, hurry!"

The male coyote killed the second pup, tossed the dead body aside, and reentered the hole.

"Don't let him kill the last one!" Leah screamed.

"Last one?" Pepper mumbled.

"Shoot him! Nathan, shoot him!" Colin cried.

Nathan lowered the rifle to the hole and was ready to squeeze the trigger when the male coyote appeared, but Pepper grabbed the gun from his hand.

"Let him be, boy, let him be!"

"But he's killing them," Nathan cried. "Look, he's killed another one!"

"Sure he killed them. He's got to. He's a coyote! He'll be leaving now."

Nathan brushed the tears from his eyes and watched as the male coyote slinked down the hill following the female.

"Why did he kill them?" Leah cried.

"Don't you shed no tears, young lady. You and Colin killed them coyote pups and you know it!" Pepper barked.

"What?"

"How many of them did you pick up and play with?"

"We didn't," Colin started to interject.

"You lifted up the boards under that bunk and grabbed some of them pups, didn't ya?" Pepper demanded.

"But," Leah sobbed, "they were just babies. Just like little puppy dogs!"

"And they were hungry." Colin, too, had tears rolling down his cheeks. "They just kept crying, so we gave them something to eat!"

"But you couldn't reach one of them, could ya?" Pepper continued to interrogate.

"No," Leah sobbed, "it ran up the hole and hid."

"Well, that's the one the momma saved. The others smelled just like us humans, so they had to be killed."

"Why?" Nathan quizzed. "What's wrong with smelling like humans?"

"Because coyotes are supposed to smell like coyotes. If they don't keep those smells separate, those little ones—and the parents—won't be able to distinguish friendly smells from dangerous ones."

Pepper walked back to the corral gate and picked up the broken-handled shovel that they had been using to set the posts.

"Miss Leah, I want you and Colin to go bury those pups before Nathan's dog decides to eat them or this storm busts loose," Pepper ordered.

"Oh, no!" Leah moaned, "I can't do that!"

"You owe it to them, don't ya?" Pepper shoved the shovel at Colin.

"Would Tona really eat them?" Colin's eyes grew big as he spoke.

"He's a dog. Of course he would." Pepper shrugged. "Now listen up, boys and girls, and I'll tell you this lesson one more time. Coyotes are supposed to act like coyotes. Dogs are supposed to act like dogs. People are supposed to act like people. You forget that lesson, and it could cost you your life."

"But," Nathan added, "sometimes people don't act right. How do we know which people are acting 'people true'?"

"Mule's ear!" Pepper boomed. "That's why you go to church and read the Good Book. Ya have read the Bible, haven't ya?"

Tears streaked Leah's face and tangled with the matted hair that plastered her cheeks. "I don't know how to read," she sniffed. "But I'm tryin' to learn."

For a moment Pepper just stared at Leah.

"Well, Miss Leah . . . this old foot is kind of paining me, and I guess I'm getting a little grouchy. Don't let me upset you none. You and Mr. Woolly Chaps go bury them pups. Nathan, feed the horses with some hay from that little ol' broken-down barn and then put up the fencin' gear. I'm heading for the cabin. If I don't rest this foot, it will fall off."

Pepper limped his way across the clearing and into the cabin. The others just stared at each other for a moment.

"We didn't do it on purpose, Nathan! Honest, we didn't!" Leah confessed.

Nathan stood there for a moment. Then he spoke. "Let's just forget about it. If those coyotes had stayed around the cabin, we would probably have had to shoot them for attacking the calves."

"Yeah, we did them a favor! No reason to feed pups that are going to die anyway," Colin declared.

Leah and Nathan attacked Colin with their scowls. "Look, give me a hand with the horses, and then I'll help you bury the pups," Nathan offered.

Nathan kept Tona busy with him as Colin scooped the puppies into a burlap sack. Leah couldn't bear to look. Then

Nathan led the others and Tona north of the cabin to a deep ravine lined with large boulders.

Finding one rock about knee-high and fairly round, Nathan started to roll it aside.

"Help me with this, Colin. Let Leah hold the bag," he suggested.

"No!" Leah blurted out. "I'll help you."

While Tona sniffed and barked at the sack and Colin held it at arm's length as if it were poison, Leah and Nathan rolled the rock a couple of feet from its resting place. Then Nathan began to dig a hole one foot wide. When the hole was two and a half feet deep, he took the sack from Colin's hand and dropped it into the hole.

Then he scooped the dirt back into the hole and tamped it down with the shovel. It was almost dark when Nathan and Colin rolled the big boulder back on top of the little grave.

"What did you do that for?" Leah pointed at the rock.

"'Cause I don't want any animal digging up their remains," Nathan informed her. Then he hunted in the rocks and found a black jagged piece of stone. With it he scratched three straight lines in the big boulder.

"Think of it as a tombstone," he said.

"Let's get into the cabin," Colin complained. "I'm getting cold."

"Wait," Leah called, "is that it? Ain't we supposed to have a funeral or somethin'?"

"You mean, like with a preacher and everything?" Nathan asked.

"Couldn't we do somethin' . . . you know, religious?" she asked looking straight at Nathan.

"I, eh, I mean, I don't know what you do at a coyote grave," Nathan stammered.

"We have to do something!" Leah insisted. "Nathan, speak a prayer. You speak good prayers."

"Yeah . . . okay, here goes . . . Lord, You know these pups didn't have to die. I mean, not yet, anyway. We just didn't understand, so please forgive us, Lord. Amen."

"God, this is Leah Walker of Galena, Nevada. I'm here with Nathan T. Riggins. I didn't mean those pups no harm. Honest! I'm sorry . . . I really am sorry," she sobbed. "Thank You very much for listening. Sincerely, amen."

For a moment there was silence.

"Ahem!" Nathan cleared his throat. Waiting another silent moment, he then spoke softly. "It's your turn, Colin."

"What?" Colin croaked.

"You ought to pray too," Nathan insisted.

"Out loud?"

"We did."

"Yes, but—I," Colin protested, "I don't have my prayer book."

"I doubt if there's a prayer in there about dead coyotes anyway," Nathan whispered. "Go ahead, pray!"

"Well, I . . . I mean—" Clearing his throat, Colin finally squeaked, "Our Father, which art in heaven, hallowed be Thy name. Please forgive us our iniquities. In the name of Thy holy Son, amen."

As they turned to walk back to the cabin, Leah hurried to Nathan's side. "What did Junior say in his prayer?" she questioned.

"Oh, about the same as us." For the first time in an hour, Nathan took a deep breath and started to relax.

When they reached the cabin, Nathan expected to be greeted by a warm room and supper sizzling on the fire. Instead they found a cold, dark cabin and a dead fire.

"Where's Pepper?" Colin asked.

"He's in my bunk asleep," Leah called.

"Well, where's our supper? And what about the fire? I'm freezing!" Colin complained. "Wake him up. This is no time to sleep."

"Let him be," Nathan commanded. "His foot's really been hurting. We can stir up something to eat. Besides, Dad will be here soon. Leah, dig through the supplies to see what we can fix. Colin, you light the lantern, and I'll bring in some wood for the fire."

When Nathan walked outside, drops of cold rain pounded his face. *I better keep that fire going all night. When Dad gets here, he'll be soaking wet. And mad . . . Lord, what am I going to tell him about Leah? You know I didn't ask her to come with us. I just sort of, You know, let her come. But really . . .*

Nathan stood by the woodpile glancing past the round pen towards the trail that his father would be traveling, straining to see any sight of a rider.

He saw nothing at all.

Colin and Leah were holding the lantern over a sleeping Pepper when Nathan staggered back into the cabin balancing a huge arm load of firewood.

"Nathan," Leah whispered, "come here. Look!"

She pointed to Pepper's bootless left foot that was propped on top of a rolled-up blanket. Nathan stared at the horribly swollen, grotesque-looking foot.

"It's twice the normal size!" he gasped.

"And look!" Colin pointed to the floor. "He had to cut his boot off!"

"I didn't hear him complain all day," Leah added. "Did you?"

"I don't think Pepper is the complaining type." Nathan pulled the end of the blanket over the exposed foot.

47

"Well, I, for one," Colin advised, "would certainly recommend that he consult a physician."

Nathan and Leah just glanced at Colin and shook their heads.

They were soon perched around the fireplace catching the warmth of the fire and scraping some beans off their tin plates. Hardly a word was spoken until they all finished eating. They just gazed into the fire and glanced back at Pepper.

"When's your dad getting here?" Leah asked. "I'll certainly be glad to see him."

"He should be here soon. But I wouldn't get too glad. He'll probably send you back to town."

"All alone? In the rain?" she probed.

"No, of course not!" Nathan stood and shoved another log onto the fire. "I suppose he'll make Pepper take the wagon down to town tomorrow to see a doctor about that foot. That way you can ride along."

"I don't want to go home. Couldn't you ask your dad if I could stay?" Leah pleaded.

"Well, I'll go," Colin offered. "I'm cold, dirty, hungry, and we haven't even seen a cow yet!"

"And you smell like a wet sheep," Nathan added.

"What?"

Leah wrinkled her nose. "Those old woollies stink, Junior—I mean, Colin."

"It is kind of lousy up here, Leah. Why don't you want to go home?" Nathan asked.

"'Cause of her!" Leah spoke so softly that Nathan had to strain to hear.

"Her? Who?" he asked.

"You know, my dad's new woman," she mumbled.

"Do you know her?"

"No, but that don't matter. I don't like her, no matter what."

"But you should give her a chance," Nathan counseled.

"Why? She'll be just like the others."

"Others? How many, eh, wives has your father had?"

"Well, I can remember five different ones, but I think there were more than that. I can't even remember some of their names."

Nathan stared into the flames of the fire. "You don't have to answer this, but what happened to your . . . you know—"

"What happened to my momma?" Leah broke in. "She went off with some carpetbagger to New York City. That's what my daddy says. Listen, don't you see? If I go home, this strange lady will be saying, 'Wipe your feet!' 'Peel them potatoes!' 'Don't you come into this bedroom when the door's closed.' 'Go out and play and leave us alone.'"

"Well," Nathan offered, "maybe it will be different this time."

"Sure, maybe this lady will be real swell. And we'll hit it off. And I'll like her a whole lot. So when she takes off and leaves us, I can cry for three weeks. No thanks, I don't need that! Look, I just want to spend four days up here away from town, that's all. Nathan, you've just got to let me stay!"

"It's fine with me, but you better save your best argument for my father," Nathan advised.

Colin glanced down at Pepper. "Should we wake him up for supper?"

"Let him sleep. He'll get up when Dad pulls in."

"I guess I'll sleep on the floor," Leah announced.

"I'm really tired." Colin stretched his arms. "Wake me when your dad gets here. These woollies make a good mattress!"

Within a few minutes both Leah and Colin had crawled into their blankets and were asleep.

Nathan peeked outside into the darkness of the storm several times. He saw nothing but Tona who slept curled up against the front of the cabin. Wrapping a blanket around his shoulders, he sat on the floor near the fireplace and leaned his back against the log wall.

He was determined to stay awake until his father arrived, but somewhere between the steady drizzle of the rain and the mournful howl of distant coyotes, Nathan fell asleep.

5

"Nathan! Nate! Wake up, boy!"

Still propped against the cabin wall, Nathan struggled to focus his eyes and his mind. Every muscle in his legs and arms throbbed. The room was icy cold. Someone was calling to him.

"Nathan!"

Leah, who had been sound asleep, raised to an elbow.

"Nathan!"

"Pepper?" Nathan called. He struggled to stand and staggered barefoot across the dark cabin to the cot.

"Son, I cain't raise this worthless foot of mine out of bed. I been trying for an hour to get over there and build up the fire, but it's no use," Pepper complained.

Nathan studied the swollen foot. It was turning purple.

"Pepper, that thing looks horrible!"

"Kind of like an eggplant with toes." Pepper grimaced.

"Do you want me to help you up, or should I go build a fire?"

"Is your daddy here?"

"Dad! Oh, no, I fell asleep!"

"I didn't see him in the cabin," Pepper continued. "Maybe he's out looking over the horses."

"Yeah! I'll be right back." Nathan ran toward the cabin door and began pulling on his boots. "Leah! Hey, Leah, wake up and get a fire started."

"Where are you going?" she blurted out as she sat straight up and rubbed her eyes.

"I'm going to look for my father."

"Is he here?" she asked.

"I don't know. I haven't seen him yet. Can you build a fire?" Nathan called as he swung the door open.

"Can I build a fire? Can you bake a cake?" She stood to her feet, still holding a blanket around her shoulders.

"No, I can't bake a cake." Nathan buttoned his jacket and then slung on his duster. "What difference does that make?"

"Well . . . I can start a fire *and* bake a cake if I want to. Now close the door before we all freeze!" she quipped.

Bake a cake? Girls!

Nathan bounded out of the cabin and across the frozen mud of the yard towards the corrals. Tona, always cautious, skirted around the fence line, keeping one eye on Nathan.

"Dad? Hey, Dad!" Nathan called. There was absolutely no sign of his father.

The clouds were scattered, with patches of morning blue sky peeking between. A steady breeze brought a numbing feeling to Nathan's cheeks. He pulled his hat a little lower and turned up his collar.

Man, if it clouds back up, it's going to snow! Lord, this would be a great time for Dad to come riding in!

Nathan returned to cabin where Leah had the kindling ablaze and was tossing on two larger logs. "This is the last of the wood in the place, Nathan."

"Yeah, I'll bring some in later. Dad's not out there. He must have been delayed down in Galena."

"He'll be riding in today, won't he?" Leah asked.

"Yeah . . . I think," Nathan replied. He went over to

Pepper's bunk and helped lift the old man up so that his feet were hanging over the edge of the bed.

Pepper struggled to take a deep breath. "I ought to shoot that horse that kicked me!" he declared. "This foot feels like it's being chewed on by a bobcat."

"Well, Dad's not here. But he should be in later. You've got to get back to town and have the doc look at that foot," Nathan suggested.

"You're right about that, son. Hitch up the mules, and then I'll go back to town."

Colin Maddison, Jr., struggled to get out from under his blankets. "Going to town? Who's going to town?"

Nathan walked over to where Colin was now huddled next to the fire. "Pepper's foot is really bad, so he's going down to the doctor."

"We can't send him alone." Colin sounded shocked.

"And you want to volunteer, right?"

"Certainly. It's my duty to help," Colin announced.

"I don't need no help," Pepper called. "You just set me at the reins of those mules. I'll pass your daddy on the way and tell him what happened!"

The morning stayed cold, and the clouds began to pile up against the eastern mountains as Nathan and Colin hitched up the mules to the wagon.

"Now I really believe that one of us should ride to town with him," Colin insisted. "What happens if the team cuts out? Or if he needs to stop and rest? It's an all-day trip. Old Flagpole might need to lie down in the back of the wagon!"

Nathan sighed as he walked the wagon around to the front of the cabin. "You're right, Colin."

"Of course I'm right. Now I'll go saddle my—"

"She'll pitch a fit, of course," Nathan interrupted.

"Pitch a fit? Who? Leah? She doesn't care if I go or stay," Colin argued.

"You're not going. Leah's going with Pepper," Nathan announced.

"Leah? What? She doesn't want to go back. She likes this kind of thing."

"Nope. She's going back."

"Why her?"

"Because she wasn't supposed to be here in the first place. It doesn't seem right for me and her to stay up here alone. And besides it's getting really cold, and you're the one with the woolly chaps."

"Hey, you can have the chaps. Look, I never liked them all that much. Leah can wear them if she wants," Colin pleaded.

"They'll look great on a dress," Nathan said laughing. "Come on, Colin, remember how excited you were to take this trip?"

"That was a long time ago," Colin muttered.

"It was four days back . . . that's when it was! Hey, this could be the most exciting adventure in your life," Nathan chided.

"It could be the last adventure in my life!" he moaned.

"I'm going to go tell Leah." Nathan walked around behind the wagon towards the cabin door. "You go saddle up her horse and then tie it on behind the wagon."

Pepper was hopping on his one good foot, trying to scoop up his gear when Nathan entered. "Got her rigged up, boy?" He motioned outside with a nod of the head.

"Ready to roll, Pepper. Leah, eh, listen." Nathan knew his voice got high and fast when he was nervous, so he deliberately tried to keep it slow and low. "Colin and I, well, mainly I think that one of us should ride back with Pepper."

"I've survived a lot worse than this," Pepper began, "and there's no reason to—"

"Well, we want to make sure you get to town. Besides, we need you to help us."

"What do you mean, help?" Pepper asked.

"You see, we need to get Leah back to town. She wasn't really supposed to be out here and—"

"What?" Leah cried. "You're not sending me back! No sir, Colin's the one crying to go home."

"As I was saying," Nathan continued, "it just doesn't seem proper for a girl to be camping out in the mountains with two boys. So you'd be doing us all a favor by seeing that she gets home safe—and, just in case you needed a hand, she'd be there with you."

"Well, if you put it that way," Pepper agreed. "She does make good company."

"I'm not going! I'm not going! I'm not going!" Leah pouted.

"Leah, grab your gear and put some food in a sack," Nathan insisted. "Colin saddled your horse."

"Well, tell him to unsaddle it!" she yelled.

Pepper turned towards the door, lost his balance, and crumpled to the floor.

"Pepper!" she cried.

"Help me up, you two. I'm breaking camp before I get any worse."

"Leah, you have to ride with him!" Nathan whispered.

"Why me?"

"I told you why! Look," Nathan added, "you will meet my dad halfway to town. If he thinks Pepper can make it on in by himself, then ask him if he'll let you come back up here to drive these cows home."

"But what if he says no?" she pleaded.

"What if he doesn't?" he countered.

"If I get stuck in town this week with some bossy lady from Austin and you and Colin are havin' a high adventure, I'll never speak to you again!" Leah threatened.

"Grab your coat. I'll carry out your gear." Nathan bent down to roll up Leah's blankets.

"I can get 'em myself, and I certainly don't need no boy to help me. I'll tell you somethin', Nathan T. Riggins—if I was God, I'd create a world where the girls got to have all the fun!"

Colin and Nathan helped Pepper out the door and up into the wagon.

"You sure you can make it?" Nathan asked Pepper.

"Yeah," Colin chimed in, "maybe we should all go home."

"I'll do just fine." Pepper tried to smile. "Missy will take good care of me. You two stay close to the cabin, gather some wood, and don't pester the coyotes."

"Maybe we'll ride out just to look at the cows," Nathan remarked.

"Well, keep the cabin in sight until your daddy gets here. Sorry to cut out on you. Lousy luck," Pepper added.

"Or providence." Nathan handed the reins up to Pepper.

"Providence? Yep, you could be right about that, son."

Leah tossed her gear into the back of the wagon and then crawled up on the bench beside Pepper. "I hope you two have a very, very boring time!" she hissed.

"Leah—" Nathan started, then changed his mind. "Listen, just talk to my dad, would you?"

"Oh, I'll talk to him, all right!" She faked a smile and then turned to Pepper. "Let's go!"

■

The little cabin, tucked against the wall of the canyon with the corral beside it, had felt quite homey to Nathan until the wagon rolled out of sight. Suddenly the mountains seemed vast and gigantic, the valley north of them incredibly long, and the clouds dangerous and threatening.

I don't even have to be here! Lord, You know I don't want to go back without those cows! Don't let me give up. Don't let me get scared. And help me—

"Nathan! Hey, are we going to ride out there and look at cows or not?" Colin nagged.

And, Lord, help me not to get mad and bust Colin in the mouth!

Tucked against the steep cliff entrance to a small box canyon, the cabin could not be seen at all from the larger valley that held the cattle. Remembering Pepper's warning about keeping the cabin in view, Nathan found a long stick and tied his old bandana on it. Then he stuck the homemade "flagpole" out in the valley at the mouth of the canyon for a signal.

Tona led the way and was soon out of sight. The boys rode in silence.

"Did you bring anything to eat?" Colin finally asked.

"No, but I have some water. Do you want a drink?"

Colin shoved his hands, reins and all, into his coat pocket. "Are you kidding? In this cold?"

Nathan started to make a comment about it being cold enough to snow when he noticed some movement in the brush up ahead.

"Hey! Look, there's one of the cows, and she's got a calf!" Nathan shouted.

"How can you tell it's one we're looking for?" Colin asked.

"She's branded with the Horseshoe-S."

Colin pointed wildly. "Look up there! Must be a dozen cows!"

"Let's drive them back to the box canyon pasture," Nathan suggested.

"Do you know how to do that?" Colin questioned.

"Can't be too hard. We'll just get around behind them and push them back towards the bandana. When we get down there, you can open the gate and I'll drive them in. We'll only take a few at a time. Dad will be impressed that we started on our own!"

"Let's do it!" Colin agreed.

As it turned out, there were ten cows, each with a calf bounding along beside her. Nathan took the right flank and Colin the left. Tona, who always seemed to know what to do, trotted between the two boys, which prevented any of the cows from dropping back.

About halfway to the bandana flag one of the cows bolted out toward the sage to the west, and Nathan's mount, showing its inbred horse sense, broke after the runaway.

Nathan just held on to the horn and let Copper run. The horse swung around the outside of the cow and bluffed it back towards the others. Finally, the cow, not wanting to submit, turned and stared right at the horse. Suddenly the cow leaped northward, but Copper was too quick.

He dove in front of the cow, and when the stubborn animal twisted the other way, Copper was there first. Nathan lost his seat on that second cut and found himself sprawled on the dirt.

"Are you all right?" Colin called out.

Dusting himself off, Nathan hollered back, "Yeah, but look at Copper go!"

The horse continued to herd the big cow back to the others, and by the time Nathan caught up to him, the cow was where it belonged.

"Where's Tona?" Nathan asked as he remounted.

"He wandered off after you dove in the dirt," Colin shouted over the bawling of cows and calves.

Nathan was surprised that the little herd stayed together all the way back to the corral. Most of them trotted right into the box canyon pasture carpeted with thick dry grass that had escaped their hunger during the summer.

Only the cow that had rebelled earlier refused to enter the gate. She stomped, bawled, and finally charged right at Colin who was on the ground waving his hat trying to shoo her into the corral. His quick exit over the fence saved him from being run over.

Nathan's horse kept the cow from running back out into the sage, but still she wouldn't enter the corral.

"Where's her baby?" Nathan called to Colin, who was by then cautiously crawling back over the fence.

"She doesn't have one," he shouted.

"Of course she has one!" Nathan called. "All the cows that we rounded up had calves."

The old cow bellowed at the horse that prevented her escape.

"Well, this one doesn't have a calf. Look in there." Colin pointed to the pen. "Nine cows and nine calves."

"That's the problem. We lost her calf, and she won't go in without it," Nathan surmised.

"What are we going to do?" Colin pulled off his hat and scratched his matted brown hair.

"I guess we can let her go, follow her until she finds the calf, and then drive them both back."

Colin looked up at Nathan. "Can we do it after dinner? I'm starved."

"No, we have to stick right with her—" Nathan started, then paused when Colin started waving.

"Hey! Look!" Colin shouted, "Tona has the calf!"

Nathan spun in the saddle to see Tona carefully herd one small calf straight past the boys and into the pasture. As soon as the calf entered the gate, the big cow turned and trotted in behind.

Both boys laughed.

"Good job, Tona!" Nathan shouted. "Shut the gate, Colin."

"Maybe you have a cow dog!" Colin laughed.

"Yeah. Maybe so. Let's eat, cowboy!"

"You said it, buckaroo!"

The boys loosened the cinches on the horses, turned them into the round pen, and bounded towards the cabin.

6

A mouse!" Colin hollered. "It's trying to dig into our grub bag! Shoot it!"

"Shoot it?" Nathan grimaced. "Inside the cabin?"

"Well, do something! We can't have mice eating our supplies," Colin insisted.

"We need the coyotes back," Nathan offered. "Hit it with one of those sticks!"

Colin grabbed a piece of broken shovel handle that leaned against the wall and swatted, missing the mouse by a foot.

It fled straight at Nathan, then cut towards the bunk end of the cabin.

"Give me that!" Nathan shouted, grabbing the stick out of Colin's hand. "You couldn't hit a watermelon in a pantry."

"Well, I wasn't really trying," Colin pouted. "I didn't want mouse guts all over our groceries."

"That's nice of you." Nathan got down on his hands and knees and peered under the bunk. "Listen. You push the bed away from the wall and stomp your foot back there. When the mouse runs out this side, I'll clobber it!"

Colin cautiously pushed the bunk forward, and he could see the tiny wad of gray hair hiding in the corner of the cabin. "Shoo, scat! Go on, git!"

"Stamp your feet, rattle the bed, or something!" Nathan ordered.

Colin lifted the the bed and banged it down on the floor.

"Here it comes, Nathan!"

"Where?"

"It's under the bed!"

"I see it!" Nathan hollered. "No. It's coming back toward you, Colin. Stomp your feet again!"

This time the thunderous stomp on the floor gave way to an ear-piercing scream as Colin leaped on the bed and danced around. "Get it off me! Get it off me! Shoot it! Shoot that varmint!"

The bunk partially collapsed under Colin, and he fell on top of Nathan, who then let out a frightened scream himself. Both boys rolled across the floor trying to get to their feet, but kept tripping over each other.

"It's up my britches leg!" Colin cried. He struggled to stand and tore wildly at the buckle on his chaps. "There it is! Kill it!"

The little gray mouse crawled out onto Colin's boot, showing even more terror than the boys. With lightning speed, Nathan slammed the shovel handle down at the mouse, which retreated up Colin's leg.

The blow landed with a dull thud across the top of Colin's foot. Colin's high-pitched scream almost deafened Nathan.

Colin now hopped around the cabin on one foot, his chaps and britches slipping down to his knees. The mouse took refuge somewhere in the folds of his trousers.

Nathan suddenly shoved the cabin door open and tackled Colin. Both boys tumbled out the door and into the yard. In the confusion, Tona stood a few feet away barking continuously.

The mouse lost its grip on the tumbling Colin and rolled out of his pant leg and across the dirt. Tona immediately gave it a stiff-legged, two-paw pounce and soon had the trouble-maker pinned to the turf.

Nathan watched Tona from the ground where he was sprawled. The dog reached down to grab the mouse in his teeth, but the little rodent, with one last act of courage, reached up and bit Tona on the soft part of his already injured black nose. The dog yelped, but clamped down on the mouse, shook it violently, and then tossed it high in the air.

When its lifeless body hit the ground, Tona was ready with another pounce, another shake, and another toss. This was repeated three times. Finally, nudging the deceased mouse, Tona changed games. This time he brought it over and dumped it about two feet from Nathan. Then he backed up and crouched down, with his rear end crazily high in the air and dared Nathan to try and steal his treasured mouse.

Nathan, having played the same game with Tona before, pretended to grab for the mouse. Tona swooped in and grabbed the little mouse and sprinted down to the corrals, confident that he had won the game.

"You broke my foot!" Colin cried as he staggered around the yard trying to pull up his britches and refasten his chaps.

"You told me to hit the mouse," Nathan tried to explain.

"Well, I also told you to shoot that little varmint, but I didn't mean while he was climbing up my leg."

"Is it real bad?" Nathan asked.

"I'll survive. But don't you tell any living person about this, do you understand?" Colin demanded.

"Hey, wouldn't that have been swell if Leah would have been here!" Nathan joked.

"Listen, it's not easy to stay calm with a mouse running up your leg," Colin explained.

"I think it's starting to rain." Nathan glanced up at the heavy clouds.

"Let's get back in and have some dinner—if there's anything left!" Colin's voice was beginning to slow down to near normal pitch.

■

Dinner over, the boys straightened up the cabin and suspended their grub sacks from rawhide lacing tied to the rafters.

"Do you think that will keep them out of our food?" Colin asked.

"It should slow them down a little," Nathan answered.

"You're sure there are more?" Colin continued.

"Who ever heard of one mouse all by itself?"

Standing at the door and watching the light rain beginning to fall, Colin turned to Nathan. "Are we going to find more cows or just wait here for your father?"

"If we got way out there and it really busted loose, we'd get pretty wet and cold. Let's stick around here this afternoon. Dad will be here before dark."

The boys went out and pulled the saddles off their horses and checked on the cows and calves who seemed quite content in the box canyon corral. Tona disappeared out into the sage, and Colin and Nathan began to scout around the sparse countryside for more firewood.

"How come you're carrying that?" Colin quizzed.

"My rifle?"

"Yeah."

"I thought we might stir up some game."

"You mean, like deer or something?" Colin asked.

Nathan laid the rifle over his shoulders and drooped his arms over the barrel and the stock. "Not deer. Maybe a wild turkey. I don't know . . . a rabbit, yeah, maybe a rabbit."

"You did bring a bullet, didn't you?"

"Sure." Nathan laughed. "I'm a real optimist. I brought two bullets!"

Hiking to the far side of the canyon, they caught sight of a pile of logs scattered in the brush.

"Colin! Look over here!"

"I wonder how they got here." Colin examined the decaying logs. "I haven't seen any trees this big around here."

"Maybe someone wanted to build a cabin." Nathan reached down and found he could pull large chunks of wood off the logs. "Hey, load me up with wood. A few trips apiece, and we'll have enough for a couple days."

Nathan staggered under the load, but he managed to make it back to the cabin and drop the wood by the door. Colin came behind him dragging a ten-foot log.

"What are we going to do with that?" Nathan asked.

"There's an axe in the cabin. We can just split it up as we need it." Colin dropped the log and promptly sat down on it. "It's getting wet out here," he added.

"You're right. One more arm load and then let's wait it out in the cabin."

Nathan loaded himself up with firewood, balanced his rifle on top of the stack, and turned toward the cabin. Colin insisted on dragging another large log. As he was reaching down to heft the rotting pine, Nathan saw a gray blur fly through the air right at Colin's arm. For a split second he thought it was Tona.

Colin screamed and jerked back his arm. His thick jacket ripped, and his arm started to bleed.

"The coyote!" Nathan shouted.

The animal lunged for Colin's leg, but this time it only got a mouthful of the sheep-hair chaps.

Dropping the wood, Nathan scrambled for his rifle. At the commotion with flying firewood the coyote dove back into a hole under the log Colin had been trying to lift. Only the animal's yellow eyes and pointed nose could be seen in the shadows of the den.

"Kill it!" Colin screamed.

Nathan picked up his rifle, then hesitated.

"Kill it, Nathan, kill it!" Colin cried.

The coyote didn't cower, but rather bared its teeth as if ready to attack again if necessary.

She's making her stand right there. She's protecting that last pup. Coyote true.

Clutching his wounded arm, the terror-stricken Colin leaped towards Nathan and violently yanked the rifle from him. "I'll kill that monster!" he shouted.

"Wait!" Nathan yelled. "Don't, Colin!"

Colin shoved the gun within a couple feet of the snarling coyote, cocked the hammer, and pulled the trigger. There was no explosion. Just a click.

"You said you had bullets in this thing!" Colin screamed. "Where are the bullets, Riggins?"

Nathan pulled Colin away from the coyote den and took the rifle from his hands. "Come on, Colin. Let's go fix up your arm!"

"Shoot it!" Colin cried. "You said you had bullets in that rifle!"

"I said I had bullets. They're in my coat pocket." Nathan pulled Colin by his good arm away from the woodpile towards the cabin.

In both fright and anger, Colin pressed, "Why didn't you shoot it, Nathan? It tried to kill me!"

"Come on, it's really starting to rain. Come on, Colin, we'll talk later!"

Inside the cabin, the broken bunk useless, Colin stretched out on his blankets as Nathan built up the fire and lit the lantern. The wound was actually less severe than Nathan had expected. Only two punctures had ripped through the coat, wool shirt, and long johns. By holding his bandana on the wound, Colin stopped the bleeding completely.

Nathan scouted around the cabin for something to use to treat the wound. "It will get all puffy and red if you don't put something on it," he reminded Colin.

"Don't get any of that stuff that burns!" Colin moaned.

"It all burns." Nathan shrugged.

"My mother uses Mr. Meriweather's Miracle Tonic. It never burns," Colin whimpered.

"Well, neither your mother nor Mr. Meriweather is here right now. Hey, what's this stuff?" Nathan stood on the broken chair and pulled a pottery jug down from where a rafter joined the top of the wall. Yanking out the cork, he smelled the contents. "Well, it isn't kerosene," he announced.

"What is it?"

"Corn whiskey, I think." Nathan grimaced. "My uncle used to make this stuff back on the farm in Indiana."

"Let me smell." Colin sat up next to the fire.

Nathan passed the jug to him.

"It's poison! That's the vilest smell I've ever—Owwww!" Colin screamed as Nathan jerked away his bandana and poured the liquid over the puncture marks.

"You poisoned me!" Colin screamed.

"Well, Grandma used to call it poison, but it's corn whiskey. I sure don't know how they get stuff like this out in

Nevada. I haven't seen a cornfield since the train left Nebraska."

"Hey, look, it's not bleeding anymore." Colin began to relax a little.

"Yeah, well, at least the whiskey is good for something."

Colin looked Nathan in the eyes. "Are you sure it's whiskey?"

"Yep."

Suddenly Colin jumped up and tore the jug out of Nathan's hand. Tilting the brown pottery container, Colin took a deep swig. Instantly, his eyes grew wide, and he spit out the entire contents of his mouth across the fire. With an explosive whoosh, the sprayed home brew exploded in the flames, causing Colin to stagger back, trip, and fall to the floor. The whiskey jug flew across the room and burst against the front door of the cabin. The entire room immediately smelled of liquor.

"That's the most horrible taste in the world!" Colin gasped.

"The cabin smells like a saloon!" Nathan added.

The boys tried leaving the front door open for a while to get rid of the odor, but the wind and rain were too cold. They spent the rest of the the afternoon around the fire.

"Why didn't you shoot that coyote out there?" Colin asked.

"Did you see where you gripped that log?"

Colin laid back on his blanket. "What do you mean?"

"You stuck your hand right into that coyote's new den."

"But it tried to kill me!" Colin complained.

Nathan stirred the fire. "Well, I think she was only defending her territory. Remember, last time you and Leah got close to her den she lost three pups."

"That's why you didn't shoot her?"

"I kept thinking about what Pepper said: 'You don't get mad at coyotes for acting like coyotes.'"

"But, but," Colin interjected, "she could have killed me!"

"Did you ever hear of anybody being killed by a single coyote?"

"Eh, no. But I could have been the first!"

"Maybe," Nathan said nodding, "but you weren't." Then he changed the subject. "It's getting dark out there. Dad should be riding in any time now."

"Yeah, it's about time." Colin shifted his position on the floor. "I'm getting tired of this camping-out stuff. What if they found a new teacher already? We might be missing school!"

"What? And skip all this fun?" Nathan laughed.

"Fun? Having your arm almost ripped off by a wild animal is not fun!"

"This story is getting better every time I hear it." Nathan dug through the grub sack.

Distant in the steady roll of the rain, Nathan heard Tona's bark.

"Tona!" he shouted.

"Yeah, where was the mutt when I was fighting off a wild coyote?" Colin complained.

The barking got closer to the cabin.

"It's Dad! He's coming in!" Nathan hollered. Running across the cabin, he grabbed his boots and shoved them onto his feet, racing Colin for the door to the cabin.

Swinging the door open, they were startled by the sight. Standing soaking wet, with mud from her shoes to her hat, was Leah Walker.

"Leah!" both boys shouted in unison.

"I fell down," she sniffed, trying to hold back the tears.

7

"Where's my father?" Nathan blurted out.

"What are you doing here?" Colin chimed in.

"What about Pepper? Is he out in the wagon?"

"Did you make it to town?"

"Where's your horse?"

Leah just stood there, with water pouring off her clothes and puddling on the cabin floor. The tears streaming down her eyes were hardly noticeable.

"Have you two been dr-drinkin'? I ain't co-comin' in here if you two are dr-drunk!" she insisted.

"No!" Nathan shouted. "Of course not. We just broke a jug, and it smelled the place up!"

Without speaking another word, she plodded over to the fire, wiped her face off on one of Colin's blankets, and huddled down to the flames.

"Hey, that's my—" Colin began. Nathan raised a hand to his mouth and silenced him. He nodded at Leah with his head. In the flickering light of the fire he could see her blue lips and hear her chattering teeth as she struggled to find some warmth.

Nathan dug through the grub sack, filled a strainer with tea, and plopped it into a tin cup of hot water. Leah didn't try drinking any, but clutched the warmth of the cup in her hands and allowed the steam to surround her face.

"Th-th-thanks . . . thanks!" Leah mumbled.

"What about Pepper?" Colin probed.

"I'll . . ." she stammered, "later. I've got to get some wa-warm clothes."

"Yeah." Nathan nodded. "Sure. Where's your gear? On your horse?"

After a slight pause and a gulp of tea, Leah looked up. "I lost it!"

"You lost your gear?" Colin cried.

"I, I lost the horse!" she sniffed.

"What?"

"I got so we-wet that the saddle slipped. Then the horse bucked, and I fell in the mud. I—I don't know where the horse is!"

"You lost the horse!" Colin shouted.

Leah began to cry.

Nathan tried to think what to do next.

"Do you want some beans?" he blurted out.

She shook her head.

"What did you want? Eh, oh yeah, clothes! Do you want to wear my extra shirt and britches?"

Leah nodded her head.

"Yeah, okay, eh . . . " Nathan dug through his bedroll and yanked out his spare shirt and britches. "Look, these aren't very fancy. I mean, I had these back in Indiana, but it's all I brought."

"Thanks." Leah nodded, taking the clothes. "You b-boys will have to leave."

"Leave?" Colin exclaimed.

"I need to change clothes!" she insisted.

"But there's no other room," Nathan explained. "It's pouring down rain out there; we can't go outside!"

She motioned. "I'll ch-change under the blanket. Go down there and cl-close your eyes," she commanded.

After hiding their eyes while Colin slowly counted to one hundred, the boys were allowed to come back towards the fireplace.

Leah sat cross-legged next to the fire, wearing Nathan's shirt and britches, a blanket pulled around her shoulders. Her wet clothing hung, dripping, from a rafter.

"Doin' better?" Nathan asked.

"Yes, thank you. I ain't never worn britches before."

Nathan and Colin sat next to her.

"Could you tell us what happened now?" Nathan asked.

"Sure." Leah mumbled.

The boys waited for a moment, but she didn't speak.

"Maybe she's embarrassed," Colin whispered to Nathan.

"Maybe she's asleep!" Nathan nudged Leah, and suddenly her eyes flung open in wild confusion.

"Leah, lay back on my blanket and go to sleep," Nathan suggested. Immediately she flopped back on the other blanket, closed her eyes, and was out.

"What about Pepper? What about your father? What are we going to do now?" Colin rattled on.

"Wait for her to get some rest, I guess." Nathan shrugged. "Do you see how she looked? She's got a fever."

"But what about your father? She must have seen him, so where is he?"

"I don't know," Nathan muttered as he stirred up the fire. "Leah will probably wake up in an hour or so, and then we'll have the whole story. Anyway . . . how's your arm?"

"My arm? Oh! My arm." Colin stumbled for words. "Well, yes, I didn't even get a chance to tell her about the near maiming I received from that vicious beast."

"How's your arm, Colin?" Nathan asked again.

"Oh, well, actually, it's doing nicely, thank you. Do you really think she'll wake up in a little while?"

"Of course."

Only I'm not all that positive. Lord, this whole thing is spinning out of control. This trip wasn't supposed to turn out this way. We had it all planned. Lord, it wasn't even my idea for her to come up here in the first place! Please make Leah well!

"Nathan? Nathan!"

"Huh?"

Colin poked Nathan in the side. "Do you think we better take her to town tomorrow? Maybe she's real sick."

"Yeah. You might be right."

"Really? We're really calling it quits?" Colin beamed.

That word hit Nathan hard. *Quits? I'm not calling it quits!*

"If Dad hasn't come in by midmorning, if the weather lets up, and if Leah still feels really sick, we'll head back," Nathan conceded.

"Then we'll have to turn the cows and calves loose," Colin reminded him.

Turn them loose! That's why we're up here! I just can't turn them loose! Lord, please help us.

"You know, if it weren't for the storm, we could leave right now," Colin added.

"Maybe," Nathan said pondering, "you should take Leah back, and I'll wait up here."

"That's a joke, right?" Colin asked.

Nathan sighed and nodded. "Yep. Let's get some sleep."

"What if Leah wants to talk?" Colin quizzed.

"She can wake us up," Nathan offered.

"You think she'll do that?"

"Positive."

■

He was wrong.

Once in the night, Nathan woke up and shoved more wood on the fire. But Leah was still asleep.

The next time he woke up, he heard a sneeze. The fire was dead. It was barely turning daylight, and Nathan could only see faint blurs in the cabin.

"Leah?"

"Over here," she called.

"Where?"

"In the bunk."

Nathan got up and walked to the far end of the cabin.

"But it's broken," he mumbled.

"I fixed it. What happened?" Again she sneezed. "Are you going to build a fire?"

"Sure . . . sorry about the bunk. Colin and I were chasing a mouse."

"Who won?"

"Tona . . . Let me build up a fire. You don't sound so good." Nathan shoved some kindling into the fireplace.

"Are these your clothes?" Leah pointed to the shirt and britches she was wearing.

"Sure they are. You borrowed them last night because your things were wet. Remember? Maybe your dress is dried out by now."

"I don't remember much about last night. I don't feel so well this mornin'," she said slowly. "Nathan, when I came in last night, did I tell you what happened on the trail?"

"No! What happened?" Nathan poked at Colin to wake him up.

"I didn't tell you nothin'?"

"You said your saddle slipped, you got bucked off, and you fell in the mud, so you walked back to the cabin. Then you changed your clothes—"

"In front of you?" she cried.

"No . . . of course not. You made us come down here and close our eyes."

A faint smile lifted the corners of her mouth. "I did?"

"Didn't she, Colin?"

"Nathan's right," Colin reported.

"And then you drank a hot cup of tea and went to sleep," Nathan concluded.

"Can I borrow your comb? I lost mine. Are you sure that's all I did?" she insisted.

"Yep." Nathan grabbed his comb from his bedroll and handed it to Leah.

"Where's Nathan's dad?" Colin asked.

"Well . . . " Leah took a deep breath and stood up. "Here's what happened." She paced in front of the fire.

"See, me and Pepper made it to the river right after dinner," she began, combing her long brown hair as she talked.

"What river?" Colin pressed.

"I mean, the creek. What's it called?"

"Willow Creek," Nathan supplied.

"Yeah, well, we had just made it there when, ah, you know, ah, Mr. Haley came riding up."

"Deputy Haley? From Galena?" Nathan guessed.

"Yeah, him. Well, see, Pepper wasn't doin' too good, and I didn't know how to drive the wagon, so Mr. Haley decided to drive him on into Galena." She pulled the blanket tight over her shoulders and kept looking at the floor as she talked.

"But where's Nathan's dad?" Colin repeated.

"And what was the deputy doing halfway up to this camp?"

"Well, see, your dad sent him up here to, ah, warn us." Leah took her dress down from the rafter, turned it over, then re-hung it.

"What?" Nathan demanded. "Warn us about what?"

"The reason he's been delayed is that some, eh, you know, criminal has escaped from prison, and your dad needs to track him down."

"Escaped? Who's escaped?" Colin began pacing the floor beside Leah.

"I don't know!" Leah barked. "I don't know!"

"Well, what about warning us?" Nathan asked.

"See, your dad thinks it would be safer if the three of us stayed up here rather than drive the cattle in. So Mr. Haley was riding up to tell Pepper and us about the delay." She took a deep breath.

"The three of us?" Nathan queried. "Dad knows that you're up here?"

"Sure. He doesn't mind at all," she continued. "At least that's what Mr. Haley said."

"So we're supposed to just stay up here for days!" Colin moaned.

"No. Mr. Haley said that after he got Pepper back to town, either he or Nathan's dad would be coming up tonight. We are supposed to wait for them before we start back to Galena."

"So Deputy Haley sent you back here by yourself in the dark to tell us that?" Nathan probed.

"It wasn't dark then, and I would have made it back during daylight if I hadn't got bucked off."

"What about the cows? Are we only going to take back what we have rounded up? You told him we didn't have them rounded up, didn't you?"

"I forgot to mention them cows," Leah admitted.

"Forgot? Forgot? That's why we're here!" Nathan shouted. He could see the tears welling up in Leah's eyes.

"I did the best I could," she whimpered.

"All right, all right. I'm sorry I yelled," Nathan apologized. "Look, it's just that all of this is so strange. I mean, my mother and father just wouldn't do this sort of—"

"I thought your mom was gone somewhere," Leah pressed.

"Yes! Right! That must be it. Mother must still be gone, and Dad doesn't want me tagging along when he needs to catch a dangerous killer!"

"Yes!" Leah shouted. "That's it!"

"Dangerous killer?" Colin interrupted. "Leah just said an escapee, not a killer."

"Well, I'm sure it must be serious to keep my dad away," Nathan added.

"What about *my* father? And surely mother is worried about me," Colin insisted.

"Nah. Mr. Haley didn't mention your folks." Leah shrugged.

"So what do we do now?" Colin asked.

"Let's go gather some more firewood," Nathan suggested. "Say, did you tell Leah we found her coyote family?"

"You did? Where?" she bubbled.

"I was attacked by the brute and barely escaped with my life," Colin began.

Nathan left the cabin to get wood, just as Colin began telling how he wrestled a huge coyote.

The rain the night before had turned most of the ground between the cabin and the corral into a shallow lake. Nathan walked across the opening of the box canyon with Tona leading the way.

"Tona, did you see Leah's horse?"

The dog didn't answer.

■

By the time Nathan returned to the cabin with a load of firewood, he had developed a plan.

"Leah and Colin," he called, "look, it isn't raining this morning, so I figure we should get out there and round up some more cows."

"But it's muddy!" Colin complained. "And Leah's real sick!"

Ignoring his objection, Nathan continued, "Yep, Leah's sick. And her horse is, well, lost. So she can stay here at the cabin in case Dad or Deputy Haley or someone shows up. Besides, she cooks better than we do. You and I will gather up the rest of the cows and calves and push them into the box canyon pasture. Who knows, maybe we can find most of them before Dad gets here."

"But what if we get soaked like Leah?" Colin asked.

"Then she'll have to let us wear her spare dress." Nathan laughed. "Will you be all right here in the cabin?" he asked her.

"I've been in worse-smellin' places," Leah offered. "But not much worse. You two go saddle them horses, and I'll see what we can have for breakfast. But I ain't feelin' too well."

According to Colin's pocket watch, it was 7:45 A.M. when the boys mounted their horses and rode out to look for more cows. Colin wore his woolly chaps. Nathan carried his rifle—this time with three bullets in the chamber and a handful in his coat pocket.

8

"What's that old flour sack for?" Colin demanded.

"Flags," Nathan replied.

"Flags? What do you mean?"

"You know, flags. Markers. Pepper said not to leave sight of the cabin, but he didn't think we would be rounding up all the cows on our own. So I figure we'll mark a trail along the sage. That way if we have to chase some old mossy horn back into the mountains, we can still find the way out."

"Mossy horn? Where did you get that?" Colin quizzed.

"Read it in the *Illustrated Weekly*. Do you think we should just round up about twenty head at a time like yesterday?" Nathan asked.

"How should I know?" Colin quipped. "You're the cowboy."

"Farm boy—I'm a farm boy from Indiana," Nathan insisted. "But I do have a plan. Let's ride up to the north end of the valley. Then we'll turn around and see if we can start pushing the cows and calves this way. If we lose a few, at least they'll be closer to the corral. Then next trip we won't have to go so far out. On the final pass they should all be right up here close to the box canyon."

"Is it going to rain some more? I don't want to get wet," Colin insisted. "These chaps can smell like wet sheep."

"Those chaps are wet sheep!" Nathan laughed.

■

It took the boys nearly two hours to ride to the far end of the valley. The sloping sage-covered mountains allowed the cows and calves to graze a good distance up the hill. But the steepness of the peaks kept them from crossing over into another valley. At least that's what Nathan was counting on.

Again Nathan and Colin zigzagged across the slopes, and Tona barked his way down the cow trail in the middle of the valley. At its northern end, the valley was no more than a mile across. It took another half-hour, but finally they had eight cows and six calves on the trail with Tona nipping at their heels.

"Are you sure those other two don't have calves?" Colin asked.

"They aren't complaining about any missing offspring," Nathan replied. "Not every cow has a successful calving."

A few minutes later Nathan heard a whoop and holler from Colin. He spurred his horse and galloped over to see what was the matter. Tona trotted along behind, always keeping a sagebrush or two between him and the horses.

"Nathan! I can't get this cow to budge." Colin sat on his horse facing a huge animal that seemed to be in a staring match with his horse.

"Cow?" Nathan cried. "That's a bull!"

"A bull? Nobody said there were going to be bulls out here!" Colin gasped.

"You got to have bulls. How else are you going to get calves?" Nathan asked.

"Well, yes, but I mean, if there are about one hundred

cows out here and around one hundred calves, does that mean there'll be one hundred bulls?" Colin asked.

"What? Where did you grow up? Inside a bank?"

"Sort of," Colin admitted.

"Well, there's probably not more than two or three bulls."

"Oh . . . Anyway, how do we get this one moving?"

"Let's ride back there about a hundred feet and then both of us charge right at him. He'll panic and start down the valley," Nathan suggested.

The boys rode back a ways, looked at each other and nodded, and then spurred their horses straight at the bull. Waving their hats wildly and screaming at the top of their voices, they charged.

The big brindled bull pawed the ground with his front hooves and then snorted and lunged at the charging horses. Colin's horse split off to the right, and Nathan's to the left. It was all they could do to stay mounted.

Catching their breath at a safe distance, they searched for another plan.

"What are you pulling your gun out for?" Colin asked. "You aren't going to shoot the bull, are you?"

"Nope, but just in case that old boy catches us down off our horses, I might need to convince him to change directions. I'm not taking any chances."

"Let's have Tona drive him," Colin suggested. "He's good with animals."

"Maybe . . . " Nathan pondered. "Yeah, it might work. You ride over there, and I'll stay here. Then we'll let Tona have the middle, and he can nip at the bull and drive it along."

They rode up behind the bull and spread out, leaving Tona to do his work. At first, the plan worked well. The bull, annoyed by the barking dog, started to saunter southward through the sage.

Then, just as Tona dove at the bull's heels, the big bruiser spun with lightning speed and charged the dog. Catching Tona above his left horn, the bull flipped the dog twenty feet across the sage. Tona landed with a thud on the dirt and struggled to his feet. At that moment the bull charged the dog.

Colin screamed.

Nathan lifted the rifle and fired a shot into the dirt, right in front of the bull. The big animal slid to a halt, turned to look at Nathan, and then charged at his horse.

Copper bolted down the slope for the valley floor with Nathan clutching the horn tightly in one hand and the reins and his rifle in the other. Glancing back, he noticed the bull had pulled up and stopped, so he reined the horse to the left and rode a wide circle back to Colin.

"Is Tona all right?" Nathan yelled.

"He got up, shook himself off, and ran back down to the cows," Colin hollered. "I think he gave up on the bull. Do you really think we're supposed to bring the bull back? Maybe they just leave him up here every fall."

"We'll bring him back," Nathan assured him. "Look . . ." He paused, waited, then spoke again. "Coyotes are supposed to act like coyotes, right?"

"Right." Colin nodded. "But what does that have to do—"

"Wait. And people are supposed to act like people."

"Correct." Colin scratched the back of his neck. "But what—"

"And . . . AND bulls are supposed to act like bulls."

"So?" Colin demanded.

"Well, we're making this bull act just like a bull.

Stubborn, independent, aggressive. He has no reason in the world to want to do what we tell him, right?"

"So what?" Colin was obviously getting tired of the delay.

"So what is the one thing on earth a bull is supposed to follow?" Nathan waved his hand towards the bull.

"Eh . . . a cow?" Colin reasoned.

"Exactly. So let's go down there and get those cows and calves we've rounded up and drive them up by this bull. When he sees all the cows heading south, he'll join in."

"Or he'll scatter what we've collected," Colin countered.

"Maybe. But let's try it!" Nathan loped off towards Tona and the cows and calves.

Pushing the cattle along ahead of them, they headed up the slope towards the bull. He just stood and stared as the cows trotted right towards him. The big bull faced the cows and didn't budge as they milled around him and kept going. When the last cow and calf had passed, Nathan figured that his plan had failed. But suddenly the bull spun quickly to the south and trotted along to catch up with the others.

"See!" Nathan shouted. "Bulls are supposed to act like bulls!"

"I hope the next bull is easier than that!" Colin shouted as he fanned out to resume herding the cows.

■

It was well past noon before the boys made it back to the box canyon corrals. Colin had pleaded to come in earlier, but Nathan insisted that they bring in the whole bunch without taking a break.

Colin stood by the gate and counted as Nathan and Tona pushed cows, calves, and bull into the tall grass of the corral.

"Forty-one cows, thirty-six calves, and one bull!" he shouted.

"That makes fifty-one cows altogether," Nathan announced. "Hey, we're halfway there!"

"Yeah, but we don't know if those were the easy half or the difficult half." Colin walked his horse over to the round pen and led the horse in. "Let's go see what Leah cooked for us. I'm starved!" he announced.

Both boys hit the door of the cabin about the same time. They jostled for a moment; then Colin entered first.

"Leah, I'm starved! I hope you cooked lots of whatever it is you cooked," Colin called into the darkened cabin.

"Hey, Leah, you should have seen this bull we brought in!" Nathan added.

"Yeah, it must have flipped Tona fifty feet across the sagebrush, and then—"

Nathan hushed Colin. "Hey, she's asleep."

"Asleep?" Colin complained. "What about dinner? Wake her up!"

"She doesn't look too good," Nathan cautioned. "Look how red and flushed her face is. We better let her sleep."

"Well, I'm tired too, and if she's going to pull her weight, she's just going to have to—"

"Hush!" Nathan whispered. "It's all right for sick people to act like sick people. There's still some coals going over there, so build up the fire, and we'll scout up some food for ourselves."

Nathan found a fairly clean rag and poured a little cool water in a basin. Then he soaked the rag, wrung out most of the water, and placed it across Leah's forehead. At the touch of the cool rag, she opened her eyes.

"I don't feel so good," she whimpered. "I wanted to cook, I really did. There's some beans soaking over there."

"It's okay," Nathan assured her. "Look, you just rest today. My dad will be here by this evening. He'll know what to do."

"I ain't helping very much. I should have gone to town and stayed."

"Well, you had to ride on back and tell us to stay put. Remember?" Nathan reminded her. "Tomorrow you'll feel better."

"I'll bake you a cake tomorrow," she promised.

"Don't worry about that now. Do you want us to stay here with you this afternoon?" Nathan asked.

"Yeah," Colin quipped, "maybe we should take her to town."

"It would make me feel worse if I knew I was holdin' you back. You can go on . . . if I feel good, I'll cook. If not, I'll be right here."

"Do you need more blankets?" Nathan offered.

"I've got all of them now," she whispered. Then she closed her eyes and rested.

■

After stuffing themselves on what turned out to be a fairly big meal, Colin and Nathan sat near the fireplace in the cabin and relaxed.

"Are you stiff and sore?" Colin asked.

"Yeah. Maybe we ought to stand up in the stirrups all afternoon." Nathan laughed. "I thought about seeing how many we could round up from the ground. That's the way we did it back in Indiana. But then I got to thinking about that old bull and decided we better stay on the horses. Are you ready to ride, cowboy?"

"Cowboy?" Colin groaned. "Why would anyone want to do this for a living? Me, I'm going to be a banker. How about you, Nathan? What do you want to be?"

"I guess I'll be a farmer like Grandad, or maybe a rancher. I don't know. I always thought I'd like to be a doctor, but you got to have lots of money to go to school."

"Dr. Nathan T. Riggins!" Colin kidded. "Sure, I can just see you riding in some buggy for fifty miles so you could deliver some dirt-poor woman's baby."

"What's wrong with that?"

"Lousy hours," Colin chided. "Listen, Dr. Riggins, do you think Leah's really sick or is she just faking it?"

"You don't fake a fever," Nathan responded.

"Hey, I did once! See, I put my face really close to our wood stove and then ran over and had my mother feel my forehead. I missed two days of school because of that."

"Well, Leah's sick. I can tell that. Besides, she's just not the type to lie about something important. She hasn't got a reason to pretend to be sick." Nathan's whisper was sounding more like a shout.

"Are you two goin' to go out and catch them cows or not?" Leah called from the darkened end of the room.

The boys pulled on their jackets and banged out the door.

"Well, maybe she does have a fever." Colin laughed. "At least her ears were burning!"

The sun broke clear of the clouds, and the afternoon turned out to be the most pleasant since they had left Galena. The mud puddles evaporated quickly and an almost warm southern breeze drifted into the valley. Within an hour the boys had pulled off their coats and tied them to the backs of their saddles.

Nathan found more than a dozen cows and their calves grazing in almost single file high up on the western slope and had no problem pushing them down to the others. The boys had worked the valley far enough south that they could see the entrance to the box canyon from most everywhere they rode.

Colin ran across another bull, and Tona refused to go near it. But this time they made sure they didn't get it off by itself. By keeping it with the cows, they found it would move right along with the others.

Nathan thought he counted thirty-five cows plus their calves in the present band.

"That would make eighty-six head!" He hollered at Colin. "Fourteen more and we've got them!"

"I'm ready to call it a day," Colin shouted.

"Let's drive these in and check on Leah. But I hate to quit. We've got them moved in next to the box canyon. During the night they might graze clear up to the end of the valley," Nathan added.

They were just driving the last of the cattle into the corral when Nathan heard Tona barking wildly out in the sage.

"What's he got, another bull?" Colin swung the gate closed.

"A bull—or a mouse, who knows?" Nathan laughed. "You go check on Leah, and I'll ride back out to Tona. See you at the cabin in a few minutes."

Only fourteen more, Lord. Wouldn't it be grand to have them all penned when Dad got here? Lord, help him catch the escapee. And, Lord, You know I mentioned this yesterday—could you help Leah feel better?

The small valley had only a seasonal creek that coursed down its middle. Only a day after the heavy rains, the little creek was beginning to recede. Light rain and a gradual slope had kept many arroyos and canyons from forming, and it allowed the boys to sight most of the cows easily.

Nathan followed the barking, but he was surprised that he could not see Tona. Finally, straight across the valley from the box canyon, Nathan entered a small arroyo. It was too brushy to ride in, so he dismounted, tied his horse to a sage, and carried his rifle with him as he entered the thicket.

Rounding a bend, Nathan froze at the sight before him.

9

Calving? Not now—it's too late in the season! Oh, Lord, please help me now.

A terrified young cow lay among the sage and brush attempting to give birth. Circling her were two coyotes, waiting for the cow to deliver their evening meal. With random vicious attacks, they dove for the emerging calf or nipped at the downed cow's neck. The heifer tried to defend herself with violent kicks at the coyotes. She bellowed in terror from both pain and fear.

Tona gained courage by Nathan's sudden presence and charged at the attacking coyotes. The larger one turned and dove at Tona, catching him by the neck and throwing him down.

Immediately Nathan raised his rifle and fired a shot over the heads of the fighting animals. The coyote jumped into the air, spun two circles, and then raced back to its companion. The two then retreated back into the brush a few feet behind the struggling cow.

Tona stood between Nathan and the cow, still barking wildly. Nathan fired off another shot in front of the coyotes, causing them to retreat out of sight. At that blast the cow jerked her whole body, forcing the calf out into a violent, dangerous world.

To Nathan's amazement, the cow instantly struggled to

her feet and straddled the calf, beginning to lick it clean and keeping a watchful eye for the return of the coyotes. Keeping the calf directly underneath her body, she was ready to strike out with a powerful kick in any direction.

Slinking in the brush about five feet apart, Nathan spotted the coyotes returning. He raised his gun and quickly pulled the trigger. He had squeezed it three times before it dawned on him that he was out of bullets.

"My coat! They're in my coat!" he groaned.

Nathan sprinted back out of the gully to where the horse was tied and yanked his coat off the saddle. Searching wildly, he grabbed a handful of bullets and shoved them into the gun as he ran back to the battle.

The cow had just landed a front hoof alongside of the smaller coyote, tumbling it right through a thick sage. The other coyote charged at the attacking Tona. The dog dodged to the right, avoiding the coyote's leap, and instantly began its own attack.

The bigger coyote ran away from the cow with Tona in pursuit. Halfway up the side of the arroyo, the coyote turned back and leaped high in the air. He came straight down on top of Tona tearing hair out as he landed.

Nathan left the floor of the ravine and ran towards Tona. He fixed his sights on the tumbling, snapping, clawing animals and waited for a clear shot. Tona caught the coyote by an ear, and the wild animal jerked back to free itself, providing an open target.

Without hesitation Nathan squeezed off a round, and the gray coyote staggered back, wounded, searching wildly for a place to hide. The second shot dropped the animal dead.

Tona raised to his feet and continued his unceasing barking, placing himself between Nathan and the dead animal.

Nathan just stared at the lifeless coyote carcass.

A frightened bellow from the cow grabbed his attention. Leaving Tona with the dead animal, he ran back towards the cow. Just as he staggered down the slope, the lone coyote dove under the cow and clutched the calf, ripping at its throat. The terrified newborn had no time to cry out.

"No!" Nathan shouted. "No!"

He lifted his gun to shoot, but the cow, kicking wildly at the killer coyote, missed and staggered to her knees, blocking Nathan's sight. He ran around behind the cow to see the coyote dragging the lifeless calf back into the brush. He raised his rifle to fire, and the coyote looked right at him and snarled.

He didn't pull the trigger. The calf was dead.

Nathan was mad. He was furious at the coyote for acting just like a coyote.

He still couldn't pull the trigger.

The coyote and its supper were hidden in the brush before Nathan lowered his rifle. Slightly tattered, Tona rejoined him but made no effort to follow the other coyote. The cow, back on her feet, cried out for her calf.

The calf that had lived only moments made no reply.

The cow, still terrified, stood in the same position and continued to bellow.

That was it.

It was all over.

Tona was torn, but safe.

The cow was alive.

One coyote dead.

One calf dead.

One coyote fed.

Nathan was shaking all over. Sweat ran off his forehead and dripped on his trembling hands which still held the rifle. With his mind spinning, he walked around the cow and shooed it towards the opening of the arroyo.

The cow balked, then took several faltering steps and broke into a trot, passing Nathan's tethered horse and heading across the valley floor.

After checking out Tona's wounds, Nathan mounted his horse and turned back to the cabin. He was in no hurry. The reins hung limp on the horse's neck as it wandered through the sage.

Lord, how did this happen? I didn't want to shoot that coyote! But I did. I really wanted to shoot the second, but I didn't. Why, Lord? Why did that calf have to die such a savage death?

He stopped at what was left of the creek, dismounted, and bent down to splash running water on his face. The cold creek water startled him. Shaking off a second dose, he grabbed the horse's reins and walked the animal back towards the cabin.

Nathan couldn't decide whether he wanted to throw his gun away or run back and shoot the other coyote.

I had to do it, Lord. I had to shoot the coyote. That calf could have grown up and fed some miner's family for a year. Coyotes have got to act like coyotes, and me, I've got to act, you know . . .

Nathan couldn't think of how to complete the sentence. He just walked on toward the cabin with Tona trotting up ahead. It was after sunset by the time he got back to the corral. He ignored the cabin and walked the horse over by the pile of rotting logs, scouting out the coyote den that Colin had discovered.

As he expected, pebbles thrown into the mouth of the den caused only the squeaking protest of the coyote pup.

"It was them!" he muttered to Tona. "That's the father that I shot. The mother will be coming back soon."

As Nathan walked through the dim shadows of twilight, he spotted a horse tied in front of the round pen.

Dad!

He pulled himself up on his own mount and raced toward the corral. There was a horse by the round pen. It wasn't his father's. It was Leah's white mare.

The saddle hung loosely beneath the horse's stomach. The saddle blanket, Leah's bedroll, and her belongings were missing. Some raw skin was showing on his left rear pastern.

"Looks like you got your foot caught, old girl!" Nathan rubbed the horse down after pulling off the saddle and led it into the round pen with his own and Colin's.

Struggling to tote both saddles, Nathan tossed them into the shack that served as a barn. He sprinted to the cabin, banging open the door.

"Where have you been!" Colin called out from in front of the fire.

"Where's Leah?" Nathan asked.

"Over here . . . I burnt the cake!" She brushed her slightly tangled hair from her eyes.

"Leah, your horse was out at the corral! I just put her in the pen." He noticed a large smudge across her face.

"Really?"

"Yeah, your saddle was still strapped on," Nathan declared.

"And my gear, and extra dress, and my bedroll?" she pressed.

"And your saddle blanket—they're all gone," Nathan reported as he jabbed his hat onto a peg in the wall.

"Is the horse okay?" she asked.

"A little scratched up, but sound."

"It's not all that bad, actually," Colin admitted.

"What?" Nathan quizzed.

"The cake," Colin said munching. "It's quite edible."

"I ain't never used no Dutch oven before," Leah confessed.

"Well, I certainly thought there would be a little more joy over the return of Leah's horse." Nathan laid his rifle against the wall. Then he turned to Colin. "You already ate the cake?"

"Not all of it," Colin clarified. "Leah wanted me to test it."

"Did you shoot us some supper?" Leah asked. "I heard you shootin'. I ain't going to skin no rabbit. If you want to skin it and cook it, you can be my guest, but I don't eat rabbits or cats or dogs or skunks."

Suddenly the whole episode with the coyotes flooded back upon Nathan.

"I killed that male coyote!" he blurted out.

"The one that lived under the cabin?" Leah howled.

"Yeah. They killed a calf."

"They did what?" Colin gasped. "You saw them do it?"

As Leah scooped them up some supper, Nathan told them what had happened. When he finished speaking, he saw that Leah had barely touched her food.

"Aren't you hungry?" he asked.

"I'm sick! I mean, real sick," she groaned.

"I can't believe I missed all the excitement," Colin crowed.

"Well, I wish I would have missed it." Nathan shrugged.

"Now let me get this straight," Colin exclaimed. "You shot the coyote because it was attacking a calf?"

"Yeah, and it was also chewing on Tona."

"But," Colin anguished, "you wouldn't shoot a coyote when it was savagely devouring my arm!"

"Look," Nathan tried to explain, "she was defending her

territory, not trying to take something that was ours. She had stopped nipping at you and retreated."

"Nipping? You call that nipping?" Colin shouted.

"How is your arm?" Leah asked.

"It's fine—but that's beside the point!" he argued. "Don't you see, Nathan should have shot the lousy coyote! Now it's running loose to bite us again."

"I'm still thinking about what Pepper said," Nathan began. "Coyote true, he called it. Remember? Coyotes are supposed to act like coyotes. And don't get mad at them if they do. They're just being honest. Coyote true."

Leah began to eat a little of her supper as Nathan continued. "The first coyote I had to shoot because I feel responsible for the cattle, because the baby calf was defenseless, and because Tona's life was being threatened. I had lots of reasons for killing that one."

"And you didn't have any reason for shooting the other?" Colin demanded.

"Just one. I wanted to shoot it because I was mad at it for acting just like a coyote ought to act."

"Well, that sounds like a good reason to me!" Colin insisted.

"It wasn't for me. Humans are supposed to act like humans. And wanting vengeance is not one of our best qualities."

"I'm glad you didn't kill the mother," Leah chimed in.

"Well, I'll kill her," Colin huffed. "Where's your rifle? Are there any bullets in it?"

"Relax, Colin, she's not even over there. Listen, if she tries to do anything with the cows in the box canyon pasture, I'll let you be the one to shoot her."

"Promise?"

Nathan nodded. "I promise."

"But the baby pup—it would die without its mother!" Leah insisted.

"I'm going to protect those cows and calves, but I hope I don't start shooting things just because I'm mad at them. That doesn't sound 'people true.' Anyway, did you tell Leah how many cows we rounded up?"

"Yes, it's very exciting!" she added. "Now that my horse came back, can I help round up the rest of the cows tomorrow?"

"But you're sick," Colin reminded her.

"Well, this old cabin was dark and cold all day, and I sat out on the step most of the afternoon," she said pouting.

"It's all right with me," Nathan told her. "What did you do out on the step all afternoon?"

"It ain't none of your business," she hissed.

All three were quiet for a while. Then Leah spoke up. "Nathan, do you think thirteen years old is too young for a girl to get married?"

"What?" he coughed. "Married? Are you kidding?"

"My cousin, Priscilla, got married when she was thirteen and already has four kids, so there!"

"Who's going to marry you?" Colin teased.

"Kylie Colins, that's who!" Leah announced.

"Well, if you ran off and got married, then we couldn't be friends. I'd kind of like it if we could be friends a while longer," Nathan admitted.

"We could still be friends, couldn't we?" Leah asked. "It's just that if I were married, I wouldn't have to go home and live with some woman that I don't know or like."

"Yeah," Nathan continued, "but you couldn't go to school, or learn to read, or skip rocks in puddles, or ride horses just for fun, or sit on the steps of the Mercantile chewing licorice and visiting with your friends!"

"This is the dumbest conversation I've ever heard!" Colin blurted out. "I'm going outside!"

"It's almost dark," Nathan cautioned. "Why don't you go over and grab us another arm load of wood for the fire?"

"Yeah—it beats talking about this stuff." Colin huffed his way towards the door.

Nathan put the remaining logs on the fire and then sat down. "If we round up the rest of those cows tomorrow, we would be ready to drive them to town. I wonder how long we can keep them in that box canyon corral? I wonder what time Dad will be here? What was it that Deputy Haley said?"

"Eh . . . Nathan," Leah cleared her throat, "listen, I haven't been exactly, how did you put it—people true—about something."

"What are you talking about?"

She looked down at the wooden floor. "Well, see, I'm really scared to go home. So when we crossed the—"

"Where's my rifle?" Nathan interrupted.

"What?" She looked up at Nathan searching the room with his eyes.

"My rifle. I know I laid it against the wall and it's gone!"

She stood to look around. "Do you suppose Colin took—"

"Colin! He's going to shoot that coyote!" Nathan thundered. He leaped to his feet and burst out the front door hollering at the top of his voice.

"Colin! Colin! Wait! Don't do it, Colin!"

10

Nathan raced across the rocky yard towards the far side of the box canyon. In the evening shadows, he stumbled twice and had to brush himself off and keep going. Tona was nowhere in sight.

"Colin!" he screamed.

Two rapid explosions sent chills down Nathan's back. The hair on his head tingled. "No!" he yelled and sprinted at top speed toward the log pile.

As he approached, he could see Colin kneeling down in front of the coyote den shoving the rifle into the opening. Another explosion rocked the air.

"Colin, wait!"

Tona sat ten feet behind Colin, looking at the now-smoldering hole.

Startled by the screaming Nathan, Colin stood to his feet. "Did you call me?" he asked.

"Did you shoot them?" Nathan puffed.

"Well, I certainly hope so. But, frankly, I couldn't see or hear any signs of life in there," he announced.

Nathan struggled to catch his breath. "Why? Colin, why?"

"Because, soft-hearted Riggins, there is a dangerous animal or two hiding in there. Human and bovine safety is at stake," Colin lectured.

"You can't shoot animals just for fun, and you can't shoot them just 'cause you're mad!" Nathan yelled. "You got to act more responsible than that!"

Colin crawled closer to the den opening trying to peer inside. "Responsible to whom?" he asked.

"To . . . you know, to God who created you!"

"Nathan, sometimes you let your religion interfere with daily life. Did you ever notice that?"

"Wait a minute," Nathan cautioned. "Did you say you couldn't tell if the mother and pup were in there?"

"Well, there were fresh tracks all around, but I couldn't see any sign of life. Certainly not now." He turned to Nathan and smiled.

Nathan noticed that Tona remained sitting at a distance and quietly watching.

"How come Tona isn't barking?" he asked.

Colin stood up and brushed the dirt off his britches.

"Tona? Oh . . . I guess he doesn't want to have anything to do with coyotes anymore."

"He always barks like crazy at coyotes!" Nathan insisted. "Of course if the hole was empty . . . How far can you reach back in there?"

"Reach in that hole? Are you insane? I've already had all the coyote bites I need for a lifetime," Colin reported.

Nathan got down on his hands and knees and reached into the den.

"What are you doing?" Colin hollered. "They'll rip your arm off!"

"I thought you shot them." Nathan lay down flat in the dirt so he could reach further back into the hole.

"I did—three times."

"You shoved the gun in the hole and fired three bullets?"

"Yes."

"Well," Nathan said continuing to grope, "either you killed them or they aren't in there. Either way, I can't get bit. Hand me that stick over there." He nodded.

"This one?"

"Yep. I can't reach all the way to the back."

Using the stick, he could feel the back of the den. Carefully sweeping the stick back and forth, he combed the dirt floor.

"There's nothing in here!" he shouted. "She must have slipped back and moved the pup." Nathan stood to his feet and took the rifle from Colin's hand.

"I should have brought my own gun," Colin muttered. "I never miss with a shotgun!"

"Come on," Nathan called. "Leah will be worried."

"About us?"

"No, about the coyote. Listen, take it easy with her. She's having a tough time with her dad and all."

"Soft? Is Nathan T. Riggins getting soft on Leah Walker?"

"No, that's not it."

"You going to start carving her initials on Signal Rock?"

"Come on, Colin—you know what I mean. Hey! There's another horse at the corral! Dad's here!"

The boys ignored the saddled horse and raced towards the cabin.

"Dad! Hey, Dad!" Nathan burst through the door into the lantern-lit cabin. "Did you see all those—"

He stopped dead still at the sight. Colin crashed into him from behind.

"Drop the gun, boy," a deep voice commanded. Nathan laid his rifle on the floor.

Leah Walker was huddled in the corner, and a big man in

dirty clothes held a gun in his hand, pointing it alternately at Leah and then at the boys.

"Devere?" Nathan gasped. "Lexie Devere! You—you—you're supposed to be in prison!"

"Ain't that nice—the lad remembers my name. But it was your memory that got me in trouble, boy. This must be my lucky day. I was just over there riding down that valley to Galena, looking for a place to camp, and I heard some shots over this way. If it hadn't been for them shots, I would have rode right past."

"How come you're not in jail!" Nathan demanded.

"Well, those prison guards just opened the gates and laid down. What was a fella supposed to do?" He laughed a big deep laugh.

"Leah, are you all right?" Nathan stammered.

"He ain't hit me," she replied, "but he said he would if I didn't tell him everything."

"What—what did you tell him?" Colin cried.

"Nothin'. I'm just a girl; I don't know nothin'."

"Look," Nathan's voice sounded squeaky and tight, "you'd better haul on out of here. My father's coming up any time now, and he doesn't back down from anyone!"

"You know, son, this just might be the best day of my life. Here I am, riding down the trail alone headin' to Galena to kill the marshal, and then I find the marshal's kid in a line camp and the marshal on his way. It just couldn't get better than that!"

"Look," Colin braved, "you can't threaten us. My father owns the bank in Galena, and I can assure you that—"

"You don't say. A bank?" Devere sighed. "I was wrong. It just got better! I bet your daddy the banker would pay a handsome reward for your safe return. This is sort of like discovering a gold mine."

"What are you going to do?" Colin asked.

"Well, now, I ain't too sure, but the prospects look mighty good. Yes, they look mighty good. I think I'll just wait for the marshal to show up and then shoot him. Then I'll have to dispense with the boy with the good memory. After that? Let's see, I could send missy back to town asking for $10,000 dollars for the banker's brat."

"Shoot the marshal?" Leah cried. "You can't do that! It ain't right!"

"It's only wrong if you get caught, girl. I ain't never goin' to get caught again."

"He's bluffing," Colin mumbled.

Devere moved quickly across the room and shoved the pistol right into Colin's ear. "What's that you said, boy?"

Colin began to cry.

"Leave him alone!" Nathan blurted out. "I'm the one you're mad at."

Devere backed away from Colin, picked up a rope, and tied each of their hands and feet. Finally, he had them sit on the floor with their backs to each other. He then ran a rope around all three of them securing them in place.

"You got some liquor in here? This place smells like Saturday night at the Palace. I could use a stiff drink," he growled.

"We busted the jug," Leah offered.

"Too bad. 'Course I get real ugly when I'm drunk. Now you girls just sit tight. I've got a little business outside—an ambush to set up." Carrying Nathan's rifle, Devere grabbed a big hunk of Leah's cake with his grimy hand and walked outside laughing.

"What are we going to do?" Leah sobbed.

"I wet my pants," Colin moaned.

"He's going out there to shoot my dad!" Nathan groaned.

"Did you really?" Leah quizzed.

"You would too if you had a mad man shove a pistol in your ear," Colin blustered.

"Did you kill the mother and the baby?" Leah questioned.

"Coyotes?"

"Yeah. I heard them shots, and I waited and waited. Finally I decided to come over there where you were, but when I threw the door open, there he was! Nathan, I'm scared," Leah admitted. "Do you think he'll do all those things he said?"

"Well, if he said them just to scare us, it sure worked!" Nathan pondered. "But, no, Colin didn't kill the coyotes."

"I want to change my clothes!" Colin moaned.

"Maybe if we got loose, we could barricade the door and keep him out."

"What good would that do? Sooner or later he would break in," Leah commented.

"Yeah, but it would distract his attention until Dad gets here. Devere can't hide in ambush and batter down the door at the same time. Hey, maybe Dad heard those shots and will ride up here with guns drawn. It's about dark now. Didn't you say that he or Deputy Haley would be up here by dark?" Nathan squirmed trying to loosen the ropes on his upper body and wrists.

"Nathan," Leah said softly, "I been tryin' to tell you something."

"I'll tell you something," Colin interrupted. "If I don't get out of these wet britches soon, I'll develop a rash."

"A rash?" Nathan pressed, "How do you know you will get a rash? Has this sort of thing happened before?"

"Will you two shut up about that. Listen to me!" Leah demanded. "I lied to you about Nathan's dad coming up tonight!"

"You what?" Nathan howled.

"I, you know, I lied. I didn't see the deputy down at the creek."

"What did you see?" Nathan asked.

"Will you two hold the discussion until we get out of these ropes? I really need to change my—"

"Junior! Sit still and be quiet," Nathan insisted. "Leah, go ahead, tell us what really happened."

"Well, Pepper was doing just fine with the wagon. So when we crossed the creek, I asked if he could make it back by himself. He said sure, and then he suggested that I ride back and warn you that a storm was breaking and the water rising, so we should get back to Galena before we were stranded."

"No deputy? No dad? You mean we're on our own?" Nathan roared.

"Look, I think I'm making some progress with my hands. Now if you two would only . . ." Colin tried to squeeze into the conversation.

"I'm sorry. I know I wasn't being people true," she confessed.

"But you—you lied. We were supposed to have gone home before the storm! You didn't even see anybody!"

"I say, would you two give me some help?" Colin insisted.

"We don't even know if Pepper made it to Galena. And if he did, everyone there thinks we're on our way home! Not only that, if the creek's up, then they can't get out here for a day or so anyway. How long were you going to play this game?"

"I said I'm sorry," Leah replied softly.

"If you two are through, would you mind—"

"Colin, quit sniveling!" Nathan demanded.

"Don't you see," Leah cried, "I just couldn't go home. I had to lie!"

"But when you lie, it's like . . . it's like coyotes who smell like both humans and coyotes. There's confusion and trouble if you can't tell the difference between truth and lies!" Nathan took a big deep breath and then sighed.

"I said I'm sorry," Leah sobbed. "I wish I was an old coyote. I'd just go crawl in a hole!"

"We're on our own . . . completely on our own!" Nathan gasped.

Suddenly he heard Tona barking in the distance. "Oh, no, Devere will shoot Tona . . . he tried it before!" He jerked in panic at the ropes and only succeeded in yanking it tighter on the other two.

"That's just great," Colin wheezed. "I was almost free!"

"I don't hear no gunfire," Leah offered. "Just Tona barking."

"Yeah! A shot would warn my father that something was wrong, and Devere thinks he's coming in! At least I don't have to worry about my dad getting shot tonight," Nathan reasoned.

"We've got to get loose. That's what we got to do!" Leah insisted.

"Even if we were loose, what would we do?" Nathan asked. "We don't have a gun . . . we can't outshoot him or outfight him."

"If we got to the horses, we could ride off," Leah offered. "You know, if we took his horse with us, he couldn't follow."

"I've got to change my clothes!" Colin shouted. "You two don't seem to understand the gravity of the situation."

"We have him outnumbered," Nathan continued. "If we

took off in three separate directions, there is no way he could follow all of us."

"Yeah," Leah put in, "but he would get really mad. He'd probably shoot whoever he caught."

"Are you two listening to me!" Colin shouted.

"Leah's right. If we split up, someone will get shot for sure. We should stick together," Nathan agreed. "We might not have another chance to be unguarded like this. He'll wait a long time thinking that Dad is on his way."

"What will we do then—run for the horses?" Leah asked.

"I don't know . . . he probably has the door covered. I don't know, Leah. God, help us." Nathan sighed.

"He will, won't He?" Leah asked. "I mean, just because I lied, He won't leave us in this mess, will He?"

Lord, this is Nathan. I'm scared. I'm really scared. But I'm kind of embarrassed to pray out loud. Help us, Lord. Help us now!

All of a sudden Colin pushed his feet against the wall of the cabin, kicked hard, halfway standing, then falling backwards towards Leah and Nathan. Struggling to regain his stance, he did a backwards somersault, mashing them into the cabin floor and coming out of the rope on the other side of them. He stood up, freed from the ropes around his midsection and hands.

"You did it!" Leah exclaimed.

"Quick, untie us!" Nathan commanded.

"First, I'm changing my britches!" Colin undid the ropes around his feet and grabbed a blanket.

"Colin!" Nathan shouted.

"Shh!" Colin warned. "Don't attract Devere." Then he threw the blanket over Leah and Nathan's heads.

"What are you doing this for?" Leah asked.

"So I can have some privacy!" Colin retorted.

Within minutes he stomped across the floor and pulled off the blanket. Wearing fresh britches, he untied Leah and then Nathan.

"How'd you get those ropes off before us?" Nathan pressed.

"I was more desperate," he admitted. "Now what are we going to do?"

"It's a cinch Devere will come back in here with his gun drawn," Leah added

"Yeah, we need a plan—quick!" Nathan blurted.

11

Nathan rolled one of the log rounds that served as a stool in front of the door.

"That won't hold him out," Colin whispered.

"No, but maybe it will slow him down. Colin, you guard the door while Leah and I figure what to do next."

"Guard the door? Are you crazy? Guard the door with what?" Colin gasped.

"The shovel handle that we used on the mouse," Nathan suggested.

"Shovel handle? He's got a gun! We couldn't even kill a mouse with that thing!"

"Colin, just stay by the door and let us know if you hear him coming," Nathan commanded.

"I'm going to stir up the fire," Leah announced. "I'm getting cold."

"No, wait! It gives off too much light. Let it die." Nathan searched the cabin with his eyes.

"What do you mean, too much light?" Leah quizzed.

"We might want it dark in here," Nathan muttered as he climbed on another stool and reached up for a log beam rafter that spanned the cabin about seven feet above the floor.

"We're going to face Devere in the dark?" Colin gulped.

"A man doesn't always shoot straight when he can't see." Nathan swung himself up on the rafter, lying flat on top of it.

"What ya doin' up there?" Leah called.

"Well, if Lexie Devere enters a dark cabin, where would he expect us to be?"

"Still tied up over there." Leah pointed to a pile of ropes.

"So if he goes wild, he'll shoot over there. But it might take him several moments to think about looking up here."

"Great," Colin moaned, "you just lengthened our life by three minutes. I'd just as soon get shot down here."

"No," Nathan continued, "in those extra seconds we can carry out our plan to capture him."

"Capture him? What are we going to do?" Leah asked.

Nathan swung down off the beam. "Well, what kind of weapons do we have?"

"Fire!" Colin almost shouted. "Let's toss burning logs at him!"

"Toss burning logs?" Nathan squinted and waved his hands. "How does a person toss a burning log?"

"Yeah," Leah added, "and we might burn the cabin down with us stuck up on the rafters!"

"So—what's your big idea?" Colin pouted.

"Well, I see three weapons that we could use from the rafters. There's the shovel handle, that big cast-iron skillet, and Leah's pot of beans," Nathan suggested.

"My beans? They ain't that bad!" she pouted.

"They *aren't* that bad," Colin corrected.

"See, Colin likes 'em too." She lifted the corners of her mouth in just a slight smile.

"No, I mean if you walked into a dark room and a pot of hot beans came raining down from the ceiling, it might surprise you," Nathan declared.

"Waste my good beans?" Leah complained. "That ain't right."

"That *isn't* right," Colin again corrected.

"See there." Leah looked triumphantly at Nathan.

"Look," Nathan announced, "here's what we'll do. We'll all climb up on those rafters. When Devere comes through the door, Colin will pour the beans over him, and I'll smash his gun hand with the shovel handle. Then Leah will bring that cast-iron pan right down on his head."

"Me?" Leah coughed.

"Yeah. Then Colin and I will jump down. I'll grab the gun and hold it on him while Colin ties him up," Nathan concluded.

"Why should I tie him up? Let me hold the gun. If that outlaw makes one false move, I'll fill him full of lead poison!"

"What did he say?" Leah questioned.

"Eh, Colin likes to read the *Illustrated Weekly* too. That's why I'll be the one holding the gun."

"What happens after that?" Leah asked.

"I have no idea." Nathan shrugged.

"It won't work," Colin announced. "Let's think of another plan."

Nathan looked at Colin. "What do you mean, it won't work?"

"Won't work," Colin repeated. "Now why not make a run for the corral right now?"

"I like Nathan's plan," Leah murmured.

"Listen. I'll get you two up there and armed. Then I'll shut down the lantern and douse the fire before I hoist myself up. Then we'll just wait."

Leah went over and picked up the skillet. "This one's really heavy!"

"Can you do it?" Nathan asked.

"I used one before," she said smiling.

"On people?" Colin pressed.

"One time my dad and me was living in a tent over at

Gold Hill. This gambler snuck into our place looking for my daddy's poke, so I just whacked him."

"What happened?" Colin questioned.

"I broke his nose." Leah nodded. "He got real mad and called me a whole bunch of names, and I was only eight!"

"Come on, Colin, you swing up there, and I'll hand you the beans," Nathan proposed.

"Eh . . . look, I don't want to sound, well, the truth is—I don't think I can pull myself up there. I'm kind of, you know, afraid of heights," he confessed.

"Come on, Junior," Nathan prodded, "it's time to learn a new skill."

"No, really—I can't. It's just the way my body's made. Maybe it's a physical defect," he protested.

"Well," Leah suggested, "why don't Colin stay down here on the floor. He can take the first shot, and then we'll know just where to clobber Devere!"

"Take the first shot? Now, listen . . . I, eh, I'll, you know, I'll climb up there."

"I thought so." Leah grinned.

Getting Colin on the rafter proved to be a major project. The first attempt ended with him hanging under the rafter clutching it wildly and crying out, "This just isn't working. It's not working!"

On the fourth try, with Nathan and Leah's constant shoving, Colin straddled a log rafter and clutched it tightly with his arms and legs.

"Now," Nathan said, "I'll hand you the beans."

"What? I'm not turning loose. You hold the beans."

"You can hold them and still hang on," Nathan informed him. "Open up the grip on your right hand."

Nathan lifted the bean pot into the air.

"Now close it around the handle. There, you've got it!"

"This is not going to work," Colin groaned.

"Your turn, Leah," Nathan called.

With a swiftness that reminded Nathan of how the Indian girl, Eetalah, mounted Mr. Dawson's wagon horse, Leah pulled herself up on the rafter. Nathan handed up the frying pan.

"Nathan, if it's dark in here, how are we going to see where Devere is?" she asked.

"Well, our eyes should get adjusted to the darkness, and some of the moonlight will reflect through the doorway, I hope!"

He moved the log stump away from in front of the door. Then he scattered the coals in the fireplace. Finally he grabbed up the shovel handle and handed it to Leah.

"Hold this until I get up there." Nathan shut the lantern down, and as it began a quick fade, he stood on the stool and pulled himself up. In a matter of seconds the cabin was dark.

"Nathan . . . are you scared?" Leah whispered.

"Sure. Why do you ask?"

"'Cause," she continued, "you're about the bravest person I ever met."

"You know," Colin interrupted, "it's better with the light out. I can just pretend I'm lying on my bed or something."

"No, really," Leah spoke again, "you always seem to know what to do when there's trouble. Did you learn those things back in Indiana?"

"Not really. Life was pretty simple back there. I just had farm chores, school, church, and things like that."

"Nathan," she prodded, "did you have any, you know, good friends back there?"

"Sure, there was this guy, Bradford Oakes. Did I ever tell you about Bradford? Now he was the guy who always came out of trouble looking like a hero. One time we got stuck in this old silo and—"

"No," Leah pressed, "I mean, did you ever have . . . a girl friend?"

"Well, there was Melissa. Not really a girlfriend. Just a good friend. We had a lot of fun. You remind me a lot of her."

"Is she . . . you know—pretty?"

"Melissa? Bradford thought so. You know, the only time he and I ever got in a fistfight was over Melissa. I called her skinny, and he punched me in the nose."

"What did you do?"

"I gave him a black eye! But the fight didn't last too long."

"How come?"

"We got tired of fighting and decided to go fishing."

"Do you ever write her letters?" she asked.

"Melissa? No. I don't have anything to say."

"When I learn to write, I'm going to write to Kylie Colins," she announced.

"You know," Colin interrupted, "this stuff is pretty good."

"What stuff?" Nathan asked.

"Leah's beans."

"You're eating the beans!" Nathan moaned.

"Yeah. And they're getting cold. Do you two want some?" he offered.

"When do you think Devere will be coming back?" Leah asked.

"Well, it should be soon. I mean, he'll want to get something to eat and check on his prisoners, even if he doesn't give up on the ambush. Are you two ready?"

"Yeah, but I hope he gets in here soon. My foot's going to sleep," Colin mumbled.

"If he doesn't come soon, the beans will be gone!" Leah lectured.

Lord, I haven't any idea whether this will work. Help us to be brave!

"You sure you're ready?" Nathan asked once more.

"Yep," Leah whispered.

"Oh, I suppose." Colin smacked his lips.

"Hang on," Nathan warned. Then with ear-splitting loudness he screamed, "Dad! Dad! It's an ambush! Dad! We're in the cabin! It's Devere! Shoot him, Dad! Shoot him!"

"What on earth are you doing?" Colin howled.

"Getting Devere over here—what do you think?" Then Nathan began another barrage of screams. Leah joined in, and immediately they could hear Tona barking wildly in the yard.

"He's coming—get ready!"

"What's th-that?" Colin stuttered.

"What?" Leah whispered.

"Something's crawling on me!" Colin cried.

"Hush! Here he comes," Nathan instructed.

"Something's crawling on me!" Colin shouted.

A gruff voice boomed from outside the door, "Quit that hollerin' in the cabin!"

Then suddenly the door violently banged open, and in the dim shadows Nathan saw Devere fill the doorway.

Gun drawn, he stepped inside. "What's goin' on in here? You know, I could just shoot the three of you right now! Where's that lantern? I tell you, I'll shoot! Get over—"

"They're crawling all over me!" Colin cried. He dropped the bean pot without pouring the contents on the outlaw.

At the crash, Devere fired a shot towards the sound. The bullet ricocheted off the fireplace rocks and struck the opposite end of the cabin with a thud. Devere spun and fired a shot in that direction, stepping back under Colin.

"Mice!" Colin cried. "Mice are crawling all over me!"

Clutching the beam with one hand, he knocked a mouse off his shoulder with his free hand.

Hearing Colin above him, Devere lifted his gun, only to have a frightened mouse land on his face and get caught in the bandana around his neck.

Immediately Nathan slammed the shovel handle into Devere's gun hand, causing him to drop the pistol. The outlaw clutched his hand, still trying to get the mouse off him.

Nathan heard a loud "twang," and in the shadows he saw Devere collapse to the floor.

"You got him!" he shouted at Leah.

"Get these mice off me!" Colin screamed.

"I'm going down," Nathan called. "Stay there until I light the lantern."

"Be careful," Leah whispered.

"Hurry!" Colin yelled.

Swinging off the beam, Nathan staggered across the floor and fumbled to light the lantern. In the dim glow Nathan began to make out objects in the room.

Devere lay sprawled, face down on the wooden floor. The pot of beans had spilled in front of the open doorway.

Leah was staring at her skillet. She let it crash to the floor. Colin, with terror in his eyes, kept yelling, "Get them off me! Get them off me!"

Nathan picked up Devere's pistol and his own rifle which had been dropped outside the doorway.

Leah climbed down off the rafter and peeked at the unconscious Devere.

"Colin, come on down," Nathan called. "There aren't any more mice."

"I can feel them! They're crawling all over me," he insisted.

"Leah, tell Colin there aren't any more mice up there."

Nathan gathered up the rope.

"Come down, Colin. There aren't any mice in here," she coaxed.

"Really? You're being honest?"

"People true." She nodded.

"All right, I'll just—" Colin's grip on the rafter slipped; he crashed to the floor, landing on his feet. Stumbling back, he fell down and jammed out his hand to brace the fall. "Oh no! What is this?" He stared at the gooey dark substance all over his hand.

"Smashed mice." Leah giggled.

"Beans," Nathan corrected. "Remember, you dropped the whole pot before Devere came underneath us!"

"Well, I had those mice all over me. I was almost eaten alive!"

"I think they were really after the beans," Leah commented.

"Come on, Colin, let's tie him up. Leah, you hold the gun on him."

"What if he wakes up?" she asked nervously.

"Hit him with the frying pan!" Nathan smiled. "You really clobbered him."

"I thought he was going towards the door, but he sort of, you know, walked right into the frying pan."

They worked quickly to tie Devere's hands at the wrists behind his back. Then they tied his feet at the ankles. Next they wrapped a long coil of rope around his legs, and finally by propping him up, they yanked a tight rope around his arms and upper body. Then they laid him back down.

"Well, now what do we do?" Leah asked.

"I say we hang him!" Colin beamed.

12

*H*ang him? He's joking, isn't he?" Leah asked.

"Junior? Nah. He's serious." Nathan sighed. "But don't worry, there's not a tree for miles!"

For the next several minutes they talked very little. Leah cleaned the cabin while Colin built up the fire. Nathan went out and put Devere's horse into the round pen with the others. Tona guarded the new horse as if it were going to escape.

When he came back in, he noticed that the outlaw had been rolled over into the corner of the cabin. He was mumbling something muffled by the bandana that was now tied around his mouth.

"He came to?" Nathan asked.

"Yeah." Colin scowled. "But he wasn't very happy."

"He said some nasty things!" Leah added. "So we thought the bandana would help."

Nathan glanced over at Devere. "Well, he's not exactly quiet."

"But this way we don't have to hear the words." Leah nodded.

They pulled the stools up to the fire and began to eat what was left of the cake and the beans that didn't spill out of the pot.

"Really, Nathan, what are we going to do with him?" Leah pressed.

"Well, we sure can't untie him, so we'll have to start back to town at daylight, I guess."

"How about the cows?" Colin asked.

"Yeah, I've been considering that," Nathan said pondering. "If we had those last cows rounded up, then we'd take Devere and the whole herd back to town at the same time."

"You really think we could do that?" Leah quizzed.

"We couldn't keep him tied up for two whole days. A person would need to eat and things like that," Colin proclaimed. "So I think we should just hang him, and then we don't have to worry."

Over in the corner Devere shouted something that sounded like a curse.

"I don't think he liked the idea," Leah remarked.

"It doesn't matter because we don't have all the cows and calves anyway," Colin stated.

"Okay . . . here's a plan," Nathan said softly. "We'll take turns guarding Devere tonight. Then right before daylight, I'll take Tona out, and we'll see if we can find any of the rest of the cows. Then we'll load up and take all the cows and calves we have back to town."

"With him?" Colin pointed to Devere.

"Yeah, we'll just have to take it one step at a time." Nathan shrugged. "God, help us."

"Nathan," Leah asked, "when we was up on them rafters in the dark . . . did you pray?"

"Yes," Nathan admitted.

"So did I," Leah continued. "But I'm glad you prayed. I don't think God listened to me."

"Why do you say that?" Nathan looked into Leah's eyes.

"'Cause, you know . . . I don't think He listens to liars like me," she whispered.

"I think God forgave you when you said you were sorry," Nathan assured her. "Of course He listened to you."

"Are you sure?"

"Yep. Ask Colin," Nathan suggested.

"Is that right, Junior, I mean, Colin?"

"Well, you certainly aren't going to drag me into this theological controversy," he puffed.

"What'd he say?" Leah turned to Nathan.

"He said he didn't know." Nathan laughed.

Nathan took the first shift at watching Devere. It wasn't a difficult task. Within thirty minutes both he and the outlaw fell asleep.

Sometime in the middle of the night Nathan woke up and tried to stir Colin to take his turn. Colin Maddison, Jr., (with two *d*'s) made it quite clear that he was not waking up for any purpose whatever.

Finally, Nathan nudged Leah, and she took her turn. With a blanket wrapped around her shoulders and Nathan's rifle in her lap, she watched Devere.

It was just before daylight when Leah poked Nathan.

"Nathan," she whispered, "it's gonna break daylight soon. You wanna go look for them cows?"

Nathan pulled on his boots, stood up, and jammed on his hat before he woke up enough to remember where he was.

"How did it go?" He pointed to Devere.

"Fine." She rubbed her arms and then ran her fingers through her hair. "I bet I look ugly, huh?"

"Eh, no, I mean, there's a smudge on your face, and your hair is a little messed up, but so's mine," he replied. "Did he give you any trouble?"

"Nope." Leah pointed to the empty bean pot. "I fed him the last of the beans, too."

"You fed him?" Nathan questioned.

"Yeah, he was hungry. I made him promise not to say nasty things, and I would feed him."

"You mean you sat there and shoveled food into his mouth?"

"Sure. I used to do the same thing for my little brother."

"Little brother? You have a little brother?" Nathan shook his head.

"Not no more. He died of pneumonia two years ago." She looked away from Nathan.

"But you never . . . I mean, I didn't know . . . " Nathan fumbled for words.

"There's lots of things you don't know about me, Nathan T. Riggins!" Leah confessed.

"Well, eh, did Devere hold still for you?"

"Sort of," she added.

"What did he say?" Nathan grilled.

Leah stood up and twirled around. "See, I rinsed out my dress and dried it by the fire. You can have your britches back."

"Sure, but what did Devere say?"

"He said that if I'd untie him, he would ride out of here and leave us alone."

"What else?"

"He said there were some pretty store-bought dresses down at the Mercantile that he would buy me, and he'd leave me a big box of peppermints if I'd just help him."

"What did you tell him?"

Leah grinned. "I told him he was lyin', and I ought to know 'cause I used to be pretty good at lyin' myself. I ain't gonna lie no more, Nathan. Really, I ain't!"

While Colin and Leah packed up things in the cabin and watched Devere, Nathan and Tona went out to look for the other cows. The eastern sky was barely turning blue when he left the cabin. Tona's barking had encouraged him to hurry out.

To his surprise, Nathan noticed at least a dozen cows and some calves milling immediately outside the box canyon pasture.

"Tona, are these cows trying to escape? Good boy, you kept them from getting away!"

The cows inside the corral bellowed, only to be answered by the ones outside.

"Let's get them back inside and then go look for those others—wait!"

Nathan ran to the only gate into the pasture and found it was secure. *But where did they get through the fence?*

He climbed up on the fence and hurriedly tried to count just the cows. *Eighty-six? They're all still here! But . . . these are the others!*

"Tona! These cows must have heard the others and wandered in during the night! There's sixteen cows here! That makes one hundred and two! Dad said around one hundred! We did it! We can drive the whole herd back!"

Nathan opened the gate, and with Tona's help, he pushed sixteen cows and fifteen calves into the box canyon pasture. Then he ran back to the cabin.

"Leah! Colin! Hey, the cows came in on their own! We have them all! Let's saddle up!" he shouted.

"It's still rather dark out there. Don't you think we should wait until a more opportune hour?" Colin proposed.

"What did he say?" Leah asked.

"He said, 'Let's ride!'" Nathan laughed. "Come on, Colin, let's get all the horses saddled!"

The boys saddled the four horses and tied them in front of the cabin. They grabbed some cold biscuits and jerky for a quick breakfast. The morning was cold, but clear, and Nathan sensed that it would be a mild fall day. The mud in the yard had dried, but it wasn't dusty yet. He helped Colin and Leah tie their gear to the saddles. Although it had been brought up in Pepper's wagon, most of the food that was left fit into their bedrolls.

"We just leave the cabin like this?" Colin questioned. "Don't we lock it up or something?"

"Nope," Nathan advised. "Someone might need a little shelter during the winter. I imagine the winter winds get cold up here."

"They get free lodging?" Colin complained.

"Junior! You act like you're still in Chicago! This is the West. You always give folks a place to stay!" Leah corrected him.

"Unless it's Devere," Colin reminded them. "How are we going to mount him?"

"We'll have to untie his feet, I guess," Nathan answered.

"What if he runs away?" Leah asked.

"We'll keep a lunge line on him. If he tries to run, we'll jerk him down," Nathan decided.

The plan sounded good, but Devere refused to climb into the saddle. He did try to break towards the corrals, but the end of the rope tied hard and fast to Nathan's saddle horn held him.

"What do we do now?" Leah asked.

"I told you we should have hung him," Colin hollered.

"Well, if he won't ride, we'll let him walk!"

Nathan spurred his horse and headed toward the box canyon pasture with the rope still tied around Devere. The outlaw refused to move his feet, but when the rope became taut,

Nathan kicked his horse again. The impact almost yanked Devere off his feet. He came down running, trying to keep from stumbling and being dragged across the yard. When they reached the gate of the corral, Devere was yelling through the bandana gag.

"What did he say?" Nathan asked Leah.

"I think he wants to ride the horse," she suggested.

"Colin, bring up his mount," Nathan ordered. "Look, Mr. Devere, I'll pull off that gag, but you can't yell and cuss, especially in the presence of a lady." He nodded towards Leah.

Nathan rode his horse up to Devere whose hands, arms, and upper body were still coiled with rope. He leaned over and fumbled at the knot on the bandana releasing it a little.

"You're dead!" Devere screamed. "If you don't think I'll kill you, you'd better wise up. Ain't no batch of snot-nosed brats goin' to put me away! You little—"

Nathan jammed the gag back into his mouth and tied it securely. "Devere isn't too good at giving speeches," he commented.

"Maybe we *should* hang him." Leah nodded, with her chin slightly tilted upward.

She looks just like Melissa when she does that, Nathan thought.

Her words seemed to have an effect on Devere. He shoved his left foot into the stirrup and waited until Colin dismounted and pushed him up into the saddle.

"Well, cowboy," Colin said as he remounted and turned to face Nathan, "what do we do now?"

"I say we leave Leah at the gate. She can baby-sit Devere. You, me, and Tona go into the pasture and push the whole herd to the back of the canyon. Then we work them back out here to the gate. By that time we will have to decide which of those cows are the trail leaders. Then Leah can open the gate and lead those first cows down the trail. The rest should follow behind. Most of them have made the trip before."

"How—how did you know to do something like that?" Leah stammered.

"It worked in 'Cheyenne Steele Trails Them North,'" he replied.

"I wish I could read." Leah sighed.

To everyone's surprise, except Leah's, the plan worked. About the time the sun was fully up in the east, all one hundred and two cows, seventy-nine calves, and three bulls were strung out on the trail down the mountainside towards Galena.

Leah took the lead with several cows walking only a few feet behind her horse. Colin, once again in his woolly chaps, rode on the east flank. Nathan, with Devere trailing behind him, took the west flank, his rifle in the scabbard and Devere's pistol wrapped in his bedroll. Tona held the drag position, trotting up the trail behind the herd, nipping at the heels of any that fell behind.

Nathan took one last look back at the cabin. He thought he could see the outline of a coyote sitting by the front step.

I think there's a pup . . . yeah, she's got her pup out with her now! Lord, take care of them.

■

The day progressed very slowly, and from time to time Nathan rode up to visit with Leah. It was noon when they reached Willow Creek, which had been no more than five feet wide when they rode up the mountain. Due to recent rains it now flowed fifty feet across. Nathan had no idea how deep it might be.

The cows and calves lined up to drink, and Nathan joined Leah and Colin for a conference.

"We sure aren't going to make it to town in one day, are we?" Leah asked.

"I was thinking—if the moon's bright, let's keep right on until we reach town. I mean, I don't know what to do with these cows at night anyway."

"What did Cheyenne Steel do?" queried Leah.

"He got shot in the back just outside Ft. Worth," Colin stated.

Nathan hardly heard the words. He was staring across the creek and down the sloping mountain.

"Someone's coming!" he shouted. Instantly he pulled the rifle out of the scabbard and shoved three bullets into the chamber.

"Who is it?" Colin called.

"Maybe Devere's friends," Nathan cautioned.

"Isn't that . . . isn't that your father?" Leah questioned.

"Dad? Yeah . . . *it is Dad!*" Nathan whooped, waving his hat as a signal. "Who are those guys with him?"

"The one on the black horse is Pepper. It's Pepper. He must have got his foot fixed," Leah shouted.

"And that's my father's paint horse," Colin hollered. "My father? Why isn't he at the bank? Who's taking care of the money?"

"Maybe you're more important than the money," Nathan answered.

"Is my daddy with them?" Leah asked.

"Eh, no . . . but he might not be back from Austin yet," Nathan replied quickly.

For the next several moments everything was in total confusion. The three men splashed across the river and joined Nathan, Colin, and Leah. After a joyous reunion, they settled down enough for the trio to excitedly tell about the cattle roundup and the capture of Lexie Devere. Then Marshal Riggins took charge.

"Well, I don't know how you three did it, but there's a three hundred dollar reward for Devere's capture," he reported.

"Do we all get some money?" Leah asked.

"One hundred dollars each!" Colin shouted. "We can open a bank account and do some investing."

"I can buy my own horse and saddle," Nathan exulted.

"I'm going to get some brand-new store-bought clothes," Leah announced.

"Well, young lady, you better ride up there and join that buggy coming over the hill. There's a man in there who's very worried about his little girl." Marshal Riggins pointed across the river.

"Daddy? My daddy came looking for me? Nathan, my daddy's up there!" she cried. Then she stopped and turned to the marshal. "Is he, you know . . . alone?"

"No, Miss Leah," he responded, "there's a mighty fine-looking blonde lady with him."

"A blonde?" she pouted. "Mr. Riggins, Nathan thinks I'm too skinny. Do you think so?"

"What?" Nathan coughed.

"Well, young lady," the marshal said smiling, "I'd say you are attractively slim."

"Attractively slim." She beamed. "See there, you're wrong, Nathan T. Riggins." She stuck out her tongue at him.

He began to protest, but let it drop. "Aren't you going to see him?" he asked her.

"You mean, *them*. Yeah. I hope I don't say something stupid."

"You can do it. Just be—"

"Yeah, I know, I know . . . be people true. Well, here goes." She spurred her horse and rode across the creek.

Lord, it's not easy for her. Give Leah a hand, would You?

In a matter of moments, the cattle had been driven across the creek. Then the marshal made other plans.

"Leah's going home with her father. And I've sent Mr. Maddison, Colin, and Pepper into town with Devere. They can ride faster and get there soon after dark."

"That leaves us with the cows."

"Right. You, me, and that dog of yours are going to drive these bovines home, cowboy." He smiled. "Remember, that's what this trip started out to be."

"Yeah!" Nathan shouted. "We can do it."

Once they got the herd on the trail, Marshal Riggins rode back to Nathan.

"Now, Nate, maybe you can tell me, just how in the world did Leah Walker end up on this trip? I thought your mother and I told you that she couldn't go."

"Well, it has to do with being people true . . . which Leah wasn't . . . and I wasn't at first," Nathan began.

"People true?" the marshal asked.

"Yeah, that's what Pepper calls it. It means you're being the kind of person God created you to be. It's sort of like a coyote being coyote true."

The marshal pulled off his hat and wiped his brow. "Coyote true?"

"Yep. I'll explain it to you, Dad," Nathan stated.

And he did.